"Humor, nudism and mystery. What a great combination. Mr. Azevedo has created a character that's fun to follow while the twists in the plot leave one guessing at every turn. I loved it. I want more."

—R. Brian
5 star review, amazon.com

"It's not that often that a murder mystery gets set in Sacramento, and even less so for a gay themed murder mystery. So it is especially gratifying that former Sacramentan Geno Azevedo's exciting first novel is set practically in our backyard. Geno has a very comfortable style of writing and probably due in part because he is telling his life experiences through his character, Tony Felice. **TonyFeliceMystery.com**

You will be caught up in the adventures of this private investigator undercover in a nudist resort and his mission to solve a murder on the grounds. This is the first in a series and I look forward to reading the future books and to following along in Tony's life. As President of Lavender Library, I am pleased to have Geno's book available at the Library to represent the archives of gay life."

—Clinton Vigen, President
Lavender Library, Sacramento, CA

"*Naked Dick: the Cosumnes River Murder* follow Tony Felice, a private investigator in San Diego, who is packed and ready to head to Palm Springs for the White Party when a call from his boss forces a change in plans. A young man has died in suspicious circumstances at a men's retreat in the Sierra foothills. Since the boss pretty much won't take no for an answer, Tony changes his plans and boards a flight for Sacramento. Since the investigation will take place at a nudist event, he doesn't need to pack much.

Tony's challenge is to uncover the perpetrator at a place where it seems that no one should have anything to hide. All those naked men could prove distracting as well."

—Michael Colby
Outward Magazine

"When picking a title, authors must worry about giving the wrong impression, or that reviewers will make puns for easy laughs. Geno offers a solution: make the title as explicitly, as multi-layered and as full of innuendo as possible.

Azevedo is new to writing books, but the back cover and an inside page declare that he is 'no stranger to the naturist community.' To 'share his life experiences vicariously with you,' he has created Antonio Vito Felice, P.I. In what is promised to be the first in a series, Felice investigates a death on the first night of a nine-day 'gay nudist retreat.'

Felice also discovers that, when naked, one's reactions to erotic overtones in a situation can be somewhat obvious...to develop into a full-blooded sex scene, which Azevedo describes with gusto...this is the first time I've encountered a gay naturist sleuth. If that novelty intrigues you, why not try *Naked Dick?*"

—Tim Forcer
H&E Naturist
United Kingdom

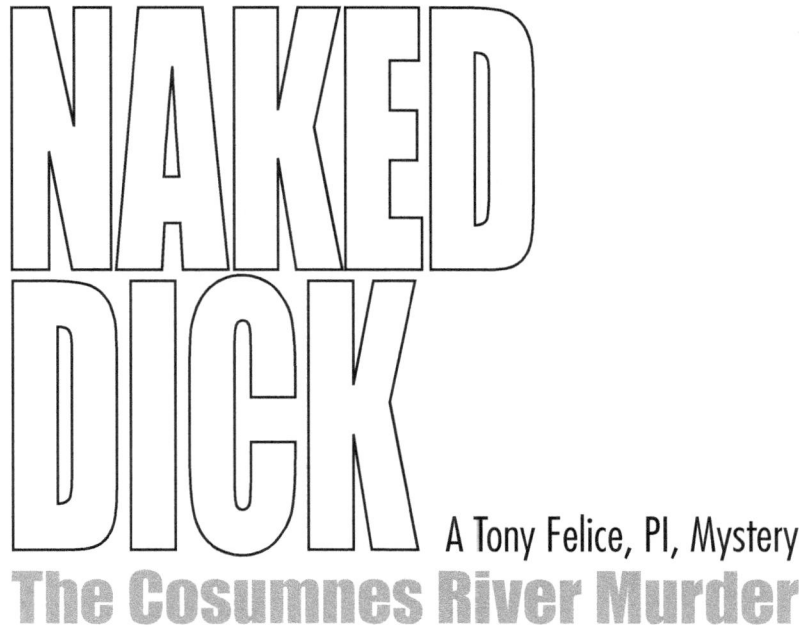

# NAKED DICK

## A Tony Felice, PI, Mystery

## The Cosumnes River Murder

Geno Azevedo

**NAKED DICK**
**The Cosumnes River Murder**

Copyright © 2009 by Geno Azevedo

A Tony Felice, PI, Mystery
www.TonyFeliceMystery.com

Design and layout by Mark E. Anderson
www.AquaZebra.com

Front cover photo by Kurt Kihlman
Kurtis-james@earthlink.net

Print on Demand by Lightning Source
A division of Ingram Books

Azevedo Publishing Company
Palm Springs, CA

ISBN: 978-1-4276-4316-2 (sc)

Library of Congress Control Number: 2011911706

Printed in the United States of America

Second Edition
First Printing, July 2011

# Dedication

To my beloved Kerry,
my partner in life
who before passing away,
always encouraged me
to write a book.

This is for you Kerry!

# Disclaimer

This book is a work of fiction. The characters, incidents, and dialogue are drawn from the author's imagination and are not to be construed as real. Any resemblance to actual events or persons, living or dead, is entirely coincidental.

# About the Author

Geno is no stranger to the naturist community and he has chosen to share his life experiences vicariously with you through the character of Antonio Vito Felice, PI. This is his debut as an Author.

He is a native Californian who worked for many years in Public Service employment before his retirement to Palm Springs. The desert sun provides ample opportunity to enjoy life with little or no textile confinement and writing is a good pastime.

Watch for more Tony Felice, PI mystery books to follow. You'll get caught up in his adventurous life and eagerly anticipate the release of the next book in the series.

# Contents

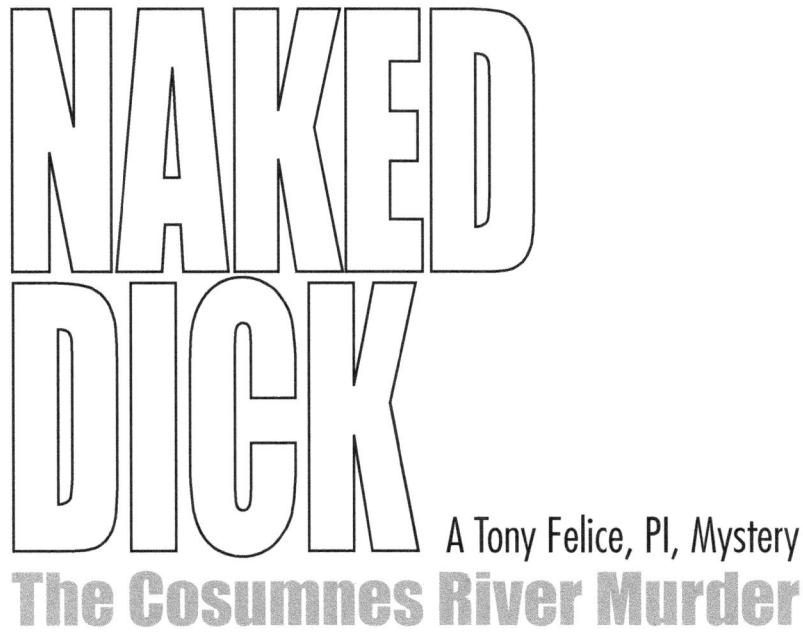

# NAKED DICK

# DICK

A Tony Felice, PI, Mystery

## The Cosumnes River Murder

Geno Azevedo

# 1

# A Blocked Call

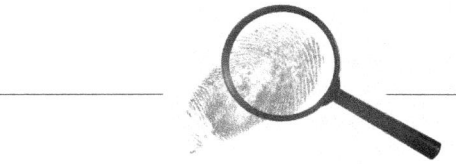

It was another balmy evening, with just a hint of a breeze as I walked home to my condo in the Hillcrest. I love evenings in San Diego and the subtle smell of the ocean in the air.

Living in the quaint gay enclave of Hillcrest is perfect for me, with its many chic restaurants and a variety of fun bars and clubs to frequent. Everything is within walking distance so I avoid the parking problem that can be a nightmare for visitors.

My vacation had started as of five o'clock and I was so looking forward to the fun-filled week ahead of me. Any time I can go to Palm Springs is special for me, but this was 'White Party' week. I've never been able to attend in the past due to work schedule conflicts and financial constraints. Now, I was feeling like a kid the night before a vacation to Disneyland. From what I hear of the week long event, the small town is filled with chiseled, sexy, tan men with hot bods, from all over the world, with everyone in a party mood.

I joined my friends as I did most Fridays for after-five drinks on the patio bar at the Park Manor. The view from the top of the Park is awesome, the sun setting on the ocean and the commercial planes approaching the San Diego Airport runway. As always it was a jovial event and the boys were out in force enjoying the warm evening. So many attractive men all dressed in their khaki cargo shorts and aloha shirts. The bar was filled with many of my friends as usual, and a few ex-boyfriends as well.

Then I saw him. The one face in the crowd that could make my stomach knot up. Brad, my most recent bf—for whom I continued to carry a giant searing torch. He'd dumped me and I was still trying to get over him. It had already been nine months, but I doubt I'd ever fully recover from that love affair.

Brad was my ideal man, slightly taller than me at 5' 10" with a muscled body and moderately hairy chest. His long curly brown hair and his hazel eyes always resulted in a tightening in my groin, and the fact that we were split up now didn't change things. Besides having a good friendship, we had a great sex life. I tossed him a gracious and casual hello, with a slight embrace, and then decided it was best if I moved on.

The evening seemed to be slipping away and I wanted to stay longer and have another Cosmo. My better judgment told me I'd better get my ass home and start packing for the trip since I was leaving for LA in the morning. I said my good-byes to the gang, and of course that process alone can sometimes take thirty minutes or more.

As I walked along Fifth Avenue toward my condo I couldn't help reflecting on how much I enjoyed my life here. What a great group of friends I have here in Hillcrest. I am extremely fortunate. It's certainly a different pace than the San Francisco North Bay area where I grew up.

My family had wanted me to stay in northern California, but I wanted to go where the beach was warm and friendly and so were the men. The Hillcrest area of San Diego was just what I needed. A gay Mecca of sorts, with perfect weather and perfect friends. And I had a great job too—which was more than many of my buds could say at this age.

I had made this walk home many times before, but for some reason, tonight it seemed especially short. I approached the front entrance to the building and prepared to ascend to the fifth floor where my "castle" awaited me. Checking the mail in the lobby, I lingered for a moment at my name on the mail box—"Antonio Vito Felice, PI."

Truth be told, it actually gave me a chill on the nape of my neck to know that I had made something of myself after those five years of college. Granted, I haven't worked on any really big investigation cases, but "…all in good time, my pretty, all in good time!" Besides, I'm only thirty-four. I have a lot of years ahead of me in this job if I stick with it. Some day I hope to have my own PI firm and if I learn well from my boss, Vince Castillo, I just might be able to take over his business, "Balboa Private Investigators."

Vinnie is great to work for, being a very calm person who has a lot of experience to offer his staff. He's getting up there in age and I don't see him running his agency for that many more years. I would say Vinnie is in his seventies, a short stocky Spaniard with a jovial, infectious laugh. We have a good working relationship. Right now I'm content just to have a steady income and be able to hit the beach most weekends and enjoy some party time with my buds. No sense in getting too serious about life too soon, as it passes by awfully fast and I want to enjoy it while I can.

Stepping off the elevator, I made my way down the long hallway and entered my world of solitude, my home. Whenever I entered that door and stripped off my work clothes I felt like I was in my comfort zone. Tonight felt even more so, knowing I was already on vacation and for a whole week would not have to hear any requests from my boss or my associates. It was just me with my friends and seven fun-filled days of party.

I was finally attending the Palm Springs White Party after living in SoCal for nearly ten years. When my bff Patrick from WeHo asked me if I wanted to join their group sharing the cost of a home rental in Palm Springs for the White Party, I nearly peed my pants with excitement. This was a perfect situation, to share expenses with Patrick and his husband Frank, along with three other guys in this four bedroom home in the famous movie star community of Deep Well. I vaguely knew one of the other guys, Gari, who seemed to be quite the party boy but seemed like a good person to hang with.

Many times I'd see Gari out at the dance clubs and had been introduced to him a couple of times by friends. Gari's always one of the first guys to strip off his shirt and show off his hard earned six pack stomach and rock hard pecs. He's easy to spot in a dance bar because if there's a dance platform, Gari's on it. I guess if I were his age and looked that good, I'd be showing it off too. That's not for me, however, as I get embarrassed when I step out of the shower and see myself naked in the mirror. There's no way you would catch me on stage without my shirt.

Another of the house guests, Mark, I've known from my past. We shared a flat as roomies for a short time when I first moved to San Diego, so I've known him for a long time. Mark's an athletic handsome blond, blue eyed, with a very likeable personality. I've always been into eyes on a man, usually the first thing I notice about them, their eyes. Not sure why Mark remains single, and it's always hard to keep track of who he's currently dating. I heard he's been seeing a Hispanic boy named Alex for about four months now. Hmm! Maybe that's short for Alejandro. At any rate, the opportunity to share the expenses with these guys was very appealing to me, and it sounded as if everyone could do their own thing and come and go as they please. That's what's nice about Deep Well—the location is right in town so it's very convenient. I'm sure if I over-indulge, I could actually walk back to our "casa" rental after a night of partying.

It was now after ten in the evening and I was relaxed and stripped down to my boxer shorts. I enjoy my small condo and living alone. I'd had roomies in the past, but I much prefer living alone since I am such a neat freak. I can't stand clutter and I'd had enough of that with my college dorm days.

Before getting started on packing, I poured myself a glass of wine and stepped outside on my deck to enjoy the twinkling lights of the City and take another moment to savor the prospects of the week ahead of me. But...I needed to get busy and get packed. I dragged out my duffle bag and started to consider what one should pack when going to the White Party. To get myself totally motivated, I clipped my iPod Shuffle to the waistband of my shorts and tuned in on Madonna. That should get me in the mood.

As I sashayed around the house throwing together my tanks and sleeveless tees and cute shorts, and trying to decide which of my five pair of flip flops to take with me, I couldn't help the liberating feeling of being on vacation and especially knowing what fun lay ahead of me. I thought about taking a good book to read but then my better judgment told me "why bother." If I was lucky, I wouldn't have any down time to relax and read. From all prior indications of the week of White Party, this was one non-stop party week with lots of HOT men everywhere. Sort of reminiscent of Connie Francis in *"Where the Boys Are"* and Spring Break. Mind you, not that I'm old enough to remember that movie but I have to confess I've seen it just a few times. What gay man could resist that campy performance of all those hunks?

With Madonna tunes filling my head, it was just by chance, or maybe I should say an unlucky happenstance, that I noticed the face of my iPhone light up as I walked by, indicating an incoming call. At 10:30 at night I would not expect visitors or phone calls. Actually, it was an incoming **BLOCKED** call. Hmm!

"Who could that be at this time of night with a blocked number," I wondered. I'd expected to hear from the boys in the morning regarding our travel plans, but if this was Patrick calling, his number is surely not blocked, and his smiling face fills my iPhone screen when he calls. Even Frank's number is in my phone directory. Maybe it was one of the other guys calling, so I figured I'd better answer it.... BIG mistake!

"Hello?"

"Hey, Tony, it's Vince."

"Hey, Vinnie, wazzup? Surprised to hear from you."

"Yeah, well, I'm sorry to be calling so late."

"Where are you calling from—your number's blocked."

"Oh, yeah, that's cuz I'm calling from my wife's cell phone. We're out for that big awards banquet I told you about and it was urgent I caught up with you before you left town."

This did not sound good but I managed to bite my tongue and hear Vinnie out.

"I hate to do this to you, Tony, but I need to ask a favor. I need you to cancel your vacation plans. I have an assignment for you and only you."

"No can do, Vinnie. I have plans and I'm going out of town. You know I'd help you out if I could but I have plans."

"Tony, you don't understand. You're the only PI that I can put on this case and it's BIG. You crack this case open and you'll make a name for yourself.... You want to make a name for yourself, don't you, Tony?"

"But...I have friends depending on me, Vinnie, and I've been looking forward to this for a long time now. Don't do this to me!"

"Tony, before you get too upset, let me tell you that I need a gay man to go undercover and investigate a possible murder."

Damn. That did sound like a good case for me to crack and establish myself as an accomplished Private Investigator. But what about the White Party! "I don't know, Vinnie. I'm not sure I can do this to my friends."

"Tony, if these guys are your friends, they'll understand. Besides, Tony, I don't like to do this, but as your boss I can insist that you take this assignment. I know you'll thank me for this once you've cracked this case."

"Damn it, Vinnie! Shit. OK, what's the assignment? I'll change my vacation plans but you owe me BIG time for this, Vinnie!"

"You're my man, Tony. I knew I could count on you," he said trying to make me feel better about my decision. "The investigation is in Northern California and you need to get up there this weekend."

"Over the weekend?"

"Yeah, and I'll go over the details and have your flight information in the morning when you stop by the office before heading to the airport."

"Can you tell me anything about it over the phone?"

"All I have time to go into now with you is that you're flying to Sacramento and you'll be investigating a suspected murder at a gay nudist retreat."

"What? A nudist retreat? Vinnie, I'm gay but I am not a nudist! Vinnie, I don't know if I can pull this one off. They didn't train us for this in 'Undercover 101 class.' I think I'd be too obvious of a plant with all those naked men around me."

"Look, Tony, I gotta run. The intermission is just about over here. I know you can do this. Just meet me at my office in the morning at 9:00.... No, better make it 8:00 to make sure you have enough time to get to the airport. Thanks, Tony. You're the best! Ciao Bello!"

"Yeah, thanks Vinnie," I sighed, having second thoughts. "See you in the morning."

## 2

# What Does a Nudist Pack for Vacation?

I never expected to be up and packing the rest of my bags at 6:00 a.m. on Saturday, but there I was. "What am I doing?" I thought to myself.

I figured I could finish all the last minute packing and get myself presentable and still meet Vinnie at the office by eight as long as I was up by six. I kept stressing over what to pack for the Sacramento trip and what to pack for a nudist event. Knowing how self conscious I am, I wanted to make sure I had some clothes to cover up any chance I could get. I dug out the lime green and yellow sarong an old boyfriend bought me in Hawaii years ago that I'd only worn a very few times since. Whenever I did wear it, I wore underwear with it. What can I say…?

Having lived in the SF Bay area, I expected the nights to be cool in Sacramento, so I'd need to take some warm clothes for early morning and late night. Then my thoughts turned toward accessories. Should I take some of my cock rings? Do nudists wear jewelry or cock accessories, or is that considered a violation of the nudist code? Well, they don't take up much space, so I threw a couple of my favorites in my bag anyway.

I'd decided to take a cab to the office and then have Vinnie drive me to the airport. That's the least he could do. I was not leaving my car in the long-term parking. It might be just a 2005 Civic Sport, but she's my baby, and paid for too, and there was no way I was leaving her out in the open-air parking all that time.

Tossing my bag into the trunk of the bright yellow cab, I crawled into the back seat of the old Chevrolet Impala that reeked with the smell of cigarette smoke. The cab driver was a female, who appeared to have driven a truck at least part of her career. She was gruff with leathery, sun and smoke damaged skin and a gravely voice. She was making small talk with me, in which I had no desire to participate at this time of the morning. My mind was on the adventure ahead of me, and the last thing I wanted was to chitchat with a dyke cab driver. The cab pulled up in front my office at exactly eight and I could see Vinnie sitting at his office desk already hard at work.

"Tony! Come on in, Tony. Have a seat.... Have you had your coffee this morning yet?"

"Not yet, but I could sure use a cup. Let me grab some

and I'll be right back."

I was a bit nervous about the details of this assignment and the cup of coffee was like a security blanket for me. I returned to Vinnie's office clutching my cup and taking in the aroma of fresh brewed java.

"So here's the deal, Tony. You fly in to Sacramento on flight 405 leaving here at 11:10. When you land in Sacramento there's a rental car reserved for you."

"Where is this place?"

"Sacramento? You know where Sacramento is!"

"No, this nudist place. How far do I have to drive to it?"

"It's just outside of Sacramento in the foothills. Some little town called Plymouth at a resort called Rancho Sierra, I think."

"Like in Plymouth Rock?"

"Yeah, like the Pilgrims, you know! The owners of the resort are expecting you," he explained, "but they don't know that you're investigating the death of one of the guests. They think you're there only because there was a cancellation...ah, cancellation of sorts, anyway."

"With the death of Zack the first night of the nine day long event," he said, "that left room for another guest— which works out great for your undercover operation."

"Nine days? You want me to parade around naked for nine days undercover?"

"Actually, only seven days now, and besides, they're all gay men. I should think you'd enjoy it...in a strange sort of way."

"Argh!" I could feel my stomach knot up at the thought of this assignment and suddenly the caffeine did not feel so good in there.

"OK...so the resort owners are George and Bruce," he said. "Here's some cash for you for the trip and you'll have to pay George for the event once you get there. All meals are included along with the accommodations at the camp, so you shouldn't need a lot of extra money. Keep track of what you spend and I'll reimburse you when you get back."

Vinnie leaned back in his chair and lit up a cigar. "Other than that, I don't know much about this week's events except that it's organized by a group of nudist gay men from Sacramento called MANS...something like Males au Naturel, or something like that. You don't need to worry about that since you're an out of town guest of the resort."

"Vinnie, this whole thing has me just a little bit uncomfortable, you know that?" That was an understatement on my part.

"Tony, just think of what this'll mean on your resume of accomplishments if you're able to crack this case wide open. The boy, Zack, was ruled an accidental death, but the kid's parents are feeling otherwise. There was apparently some bad blood between Zack and some of the other guests so they feel there's something more to his mysterious death."

"So what was so mysterious about his death?"

"He drowned in the river. His body was found face down yesterday morning and the authorities suspect he was drunk and hiking over the river rocks late at night and slipped and hit his head."

"Sounds pretty believable to me."

"Yes, it does, except that his parents said Zack didn't drink anymore. He used to drink heavily but after his diabetes began to escalate, he quit his drinking and smoking and started a regular workout routine to try and keep his body healthy. This was about six years ago according to his parents."

"Wow!"

"Besides that, Zack was an excellent swimmer and actually spent his summers while in college volunteering as a life guard at the public pool. Something just doesn't add up here."

"Is there going to be an autopsy? That would rule out foul play."

"That was the first thing I asked his family, but for some reason...some religious reason—I think the family are Christian Scientists—they don't believe in that and wouldn't allow the County Coroner to perform an autopsy."

"Wow, how weird!"

"So...here you go, Tony—your cash advance, your boarding pass and car reservation...oh, and the directions to drive to the resort. You can use the GPS on your phone if you need to...and I think that's it. I'd like to have you check in with me every couple of days if your cell phone works there. If not, don't draw any attention by using the resort phone unless you can use a pay phone in private or something. Good luck!"

"Thanks, I'm gonna need it. Oh, yeah, one more thing, Vinnie. Can you give me a ride to the airport? I took a cab here this morning."

"Not a problem, Tony. I figured you'd need a ride so I was planning on it and filled my gas tank this morning. I've been running on empty all week."

The ride to the San Diego Airport was a silent one, as I processed all of these details in my head. What had I gotten myself into?

Pulling up to the curb at the airport, I grabbed my duffle bag and said my goodbyes to Vinnie. I felt sort of like a hooker that had just been used and kicked to the curb from a slow moving vehicle by her 'John,' as Vinnie sped away in his midnight blue Bentley. God, how I wished I was on my way to Palm Springs right now instead of on this assignment. I suddenly felt lost and alone in this airport that I had flown in and out of many times in the past. This time, however, things were very different.

# 3

## Prepare for Takeoff

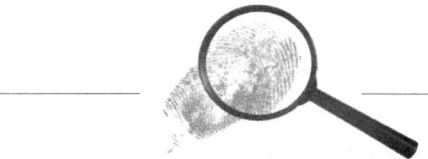

It was a quarter to nine and I was all checked in and ready for my flight plenty early. The flight was indicated as "on time" and scheduled for departure at 11:10. I figured I had plenty of time to grab a cinnamon dolce mocha at Starbucks and chill out for a bit.

"Oh shit!" With all the excitement and turmoil last night and this morning, I'd forgotten to call Patrick and let him know I wouldn't be able to join the guys for the week in Palm Springs. I was sure hoping I could catch him before I got on the plane for Sacramento.

Patrick's phone identified my call. "Hey, Tony, I thought I'd be hearing from you this morning before we leave."

"Hey, Patrick, yeah, sorry I didn't call you last night."

"No problem. We're not planning to leave here until about one o'clock or so, and that leaves you plenty of time to get to my place here in WeHo."

"No, that's why I'm calling you and sorry I didn't let you know last night. I'm at the airport and headed for Sacramento. My boss insisted I take this assignment, and believe me it's not something I'm looking forward to."

"Damn it, Tony! Why didn't you tell him you had plans?"

"I did, Patrick, but he wouldn't take 'no' for an answer. Seems that this assignment requires a gay PI and I'm the only gay agent Vinnie has working for him."

"I was so looking forward to spending the week with you and showing you the night life of Palm Springs during the White Party. Besides that, the house is going to cost each of us more now with only five guys to split the cost."

"Oh, don't worry about that. I'll still pay my share of the house rental expense since it's so late that I'm backing out on you guys. That seems only fair. Maybe I can get Vinnie to cough it up since he's the one who caused me to cancel anyway."

"Don't be silly, Tony. There's no reason for you to do that. But if you don't mind, we'll just keep the deposit that you paid us before Christmas and then we'll split the balance among us."

"Thanks, Patrick...you're the best...I owe you one. Sorry to have to do this to you and you know I wouldn't if I could get out of it. I'll tell you all about this Sacramento assignment when I get back. And I want to hear all about the White Party."

"Well, you be careful, Tony, and we'll miss you. You have a safe flight and call me when you get back in town."

"Will do, Patrick. Say hello to Frank and the other guys for me and...Patrick...THANKS!"

"No problem.... Later."

Wow, that went pretty well after all. I didn't expect Patrick to be that understanding of the situation.

Sitting at the departure gate I decided to log on to the wireless internet and try to learn something about gay nudist clubs and resorts. I figured I needed to do some homework so I wouldn't appear to be a total idiot and newbie to nudie events. That was a good thought but it was not all that long before I heard the announcement, "...flight 405 bound for Sacramento with continuing service to Portland will begin boarding in about ten minutes."

I did manage to find a web site in Sacramento for the gay nudist group called MANS and I felt sure that was the group I was to be joining. From their web page it appeared to be like any other group—organized with a President and other officers, and monthly meetings. I was able to check out some of their pictures from past events like a Christmas party and a couple of pool parties, and even pictures from prior years at Rancho Sierra. It made me a little more comfortable getting a feel for where I was headed and what I might be getting myself into. This might not be such a bad assignment after all.

"At this time, ladies and gentlemen, we would like to welcome aboard all remaining passengers on flight 405 bound for Sacramento with continuing service to Portland."

As I boarded the plane it appeared to be a full flight. Who would have thought so many people would be headed to Sacramento? But the fact that some were headed for a final destination of Portland added to the plane's roster as well. People were scurrying to stow their luggage in the overhead compartments and get strapped into their seats. Upon approaching my row, seat 10-B, I noticed my traveling companion in seat A was already seated. A handsome man about my age – could hopefully make for an interesting conversation. I had no idea how interesting the conversation would become.

Clicking my seatbelt in place, I turned to introduce myself. "Hi, I'm Tony."

"Hey, Blaine here. You headed to Portland?"

Blaine had an adorable smile with beautiful straight white teeth. His piercing blue eyes made it hard to concentrate on the words coming out of his mouth. "No, just Sacramento. Are you going on to Portland?"

"Yep, headed home after a couple of days here in San Diego."

He had such a vibrant personality. I felt I had known him for years. There was not a doubt in my mind that the man was gay, and of course that could have been part of the reason for the comfort level I was feeling. Sort of an instantly formed bro-mance. "Business trip for you, Blaine, or pleasure?"

"Sort of a pleasurable business trip I guess you could say. I'm an artist and I paint commissioned pieces for hotels and other commercial businesses."

"Wow, that is kewl. So you're working on something in San Diego now?"

"I hope to be doing a commissioned piece for the new Wyndham Hotel that's near completion in the business and financial district. I just met with the developers and decorators of the project to pitch my work."

"I'm familiar with that new hotel; it's been under construction for a while now. Glad to hear it's nearly done.... So how did the meeting go?"

"Pretty well, actually. At least my confidence level was raised by their comments. I guess they've narrowed down the field to me and one other artist from Atlanta. The next step is to run it by their Board who will make the final decision," he said. "How about you, Tony? Do you have business in Sacramento or is this a pleasure trip for you?"

"Ah...it's a pleasure trip, I guess you could say. Yeah, pleasure trip. I'm attending a retreat for a week outside of Sacramento." After my careful wording I figured Blaine would think it was a Christian Retreat I was attending and that would be the end of the conversation, but I was wrong.

"Really...a retreat outside of Sacramento? Is that in the

foothills outside of Plymouth? A place called Rancho Sierra?"

Oh my gawd, what a small world. Damn! "Ah yeah, I think that's the name of the place."

"Oh, lucky you. You'll love it. I've been a couple of times in the past and wanted so bad to go again this week but I have commitments in Portland and Seattle this next week that I couldn't get out of. Otherwise I'd be right there with you."

I couldn't believe it.... All these people on this plane and I sit next to a gay nudist. Well...my undercover skills begin. "I've never gone to Camp Sierra . . ."

Blaine corrected me, "Rancho Sierra!"

"Sorry, Rancho Sierra...but I'm looking forward to the...experience. This will be my first organized nudist event. Not sure what to expect."

"Really!...And at your age! No offense, but I've been a practicing nudist since about the age of...twelve, I guess! For me it's just a way of life. I feel comfortable without clothing, and the people I meet aren't hiding behind a designer label shirt or jeans. Everyone can just be themselves and you get to know a person for his personality."

There was a pause in our conversation as I processed the comment that he'd made, and it made a lot of sense when I thought about it.

"Tony, if you enjoy Rancho Sierra after this trip, you'll definitely have to plan a trip to the Pocono

Mountains to the annual GNI Gathering. Have you ever heard of that one?"

Things were starting to get a little uncomfortable with these questions, but I think I was covering well with my ignorance. "No, I'm not familiar with that one. As I say, this is all pretty new to me."

"GNI Gathering is in the Pocono Mountains on a huge resort with 900 gay naked men for a week. It is so wonderful. It stands for Gay Naturists International. The place has a lake along with swimming pools and lots of activities to enjoy—or enjoy doing nothing at all for the week. One thing you won't need is clothes unless it rains, which is likely on the east coast in the summer."

"Wow!" What else could I say? The thought of 900 naked men made me nervous but I didn't want Blaine to know that.

"Well, I'm sure you'll enjoy the week and the great group of guys that are gathered there in Sacramento. I wish it was me."

"Thanks!"

"If you'll excuse me, Tony, I'm going to listen to my iPod tunes and try to catch a nap before Sacramento."

"No problem. I'm going to catch up on some reading myself." Whew, I was glad Blaine didn't ask what kind of work I do. I hate to lie but being a PI always generates a lot of curiosity. I think I handled this first "exposure" (no pun intended) to the week very nicely.

With my seat back reclined and my eyes closed, I began to envision scenarios that I might encounter, just to hopefully prepare myself. It wasn't long before my mind drifted back...back to last night at the top of the Park and seeing Brad across the room.

I'm not sure why seeing him had had such an effect on me, but I know I am still not over him and likely will never be completely. Our sex life was great, but there was much more to it than that. Brad was so compassionate and so loving toward me. He is such a masculine man and I always felt special by his side when we went out. I so wish we were still together. But Brad seemed to fall out of love with me and our relationship turned more into good friends and no longer lovers. We drifted apart and I'm really not sure why.

"Ladies and Gentlemen, the captain has turned on the 'fasten seat belt sign' and we will soon be on the ground in Sacramento. At this time please stow your personal belongings and return your seat back to its full upright position." That was a quick flight—just 90 minutes and we were on the ground in Sacramento. As I stood to deplane, I turned to Blaine and said, "Nice to meet you, Blaine, and have a safe flight to Portland. Thanks too for the tip on the Pocono's event. I'll have to check that out."

"Yes, please do. You'll love it. If you think about it, say hello to a friend of mine, Eric, at Rancho Sierra. I know he's there this year. Take care, and nice to meet you too, Tony."

It felt good to stand and stretch my legs, and I was thankful for the new friend I'd made with Blaine. Hopefully our paths would cross again some day. Right now, I was on a mission to get myself to Plymouth and Rancho Sierra, and get to the bottom of Zack's mysterious death. If indeed there was a murder, it was my job to solve the crime and bring the murderer to justice.

# 4

## The Adventure Begins

Walking through the terminal to locate my baggage I noticed how laid back the people seemed to be in the airport. Was I the only one who was stressed at the thought of my week ahead?

I located the baggage claim belt and my luggage popped up right away. By all indications from the signs in the terminal, I needed to take a shuttle to the car rental yard. I was amazed at how easy it was to find my way around the Sacramento airport. I've flown in and out of many major cities and this airport was by far one of the easiest to maneuver. As I walked outside of Terminal A to catch the shuttle, the early afternoon heat hit me like a blast from a furnace. Wow, I could feel the heat of the pavement on the bottoms of my feet. It must get pretty hot here. It was never like this in the North Bay growing up, but then we had the cool ocean breeze and the fog that kept things comfortable and sometimes downright cold.

I boarded the rental car shuttle and within a few minutes I was in line at the car rental agency, along with a half dozen other travelers. I noticed the car rental agent and thought to myself: Yes, this truly is an International Airport. His name was Sarbjeet and he wore a curry yellow turban. It was very hard to understand his broken English but within a few minutes he handed me the keys to my transportation, a sky blue Kia Rio, and wished me a good safe travel. At least I think that's what he said.

Checking my papers that Vinnie had given me, I located the map and driving directions to get to Rancho Sierra. It appeared to be about 60 minutes away so I set out first to grab some lunch. I was starving. Something quick would do me fine, and then I noticed an "In-N-Out Burger." Love their burgers, so that would be perfect for a quick bite. However, it was not as quick as I'd hoped. Two school buses of high school athletes and cheerleaders had pulled in just ahead of me. Watching the antics of these kids would be entertainment for me as they teased and prodded one another like playful bear cubs. Of course the half dozen or so girls with them were enjoying the attention and I found the whole thing very amusing, thinking of my high school days.

In those days, I had not identified with my sexuality, and I recall the boys being boys in the shower room and how I tried not to notice their naked bodies. I was terrified that I'd get aroused and embarrass myself, so

I learned to suppress those feelings of attraction that I thought were just normal pre-adolescent emotions.

As I stood in line to order, I flashed back on one experience I'd had at a track meet with a guy named Keith, one of the star runners on our team. This guy was really good looking but quite the prankster and completely off the wall—very uninhibited. After one track meet, one in which he took home two gold ribbons and a silver, he was feeling especially frolicsome. In the showers he got down on all fours, stark naked and crawled around like a dog, sniffing at the other guys' private parts. That got me totally excited and I had to head fast for the men's room stalls to wait for my woody to go away. I wonder where Keith is today and if he's still as crazy—or if he ever came out!

Back on the road now headed toward downtown Sacramento, I was in awe of the skyline. It appeared that Sacramento is now a much larger city than I recalled. I'd dated a guy from here about twelve years ago, but it seemed to have grown a lot in those few years. The maze of freeway connectors and overpasses and the traffic reminded me of LA—but on a smaller scale, of course. Driving by all the high rise buildings of futuristic architectural design was impressive. So nice to see the capital city of California keeping pace with other major cities. Then from the freeway I spotted the Capitol Rotunda, its copper dome glowing from the sun's reflection. It gave me a sense of pride to be a native Californian. I realized I had better pay attention to what I was doing or I'd end up in San Francisco or Fresno, heaven forbid.

I was now headed east on Highway 50 and it appeared that I was only about 30 miles from the turnoff to Plymouth, and then only about fifteen minutes away from the resort. My relaxing drive enjoying the sights of Sacramento would soon be over, and I could feel my stomach once again tying in knots. If I don't get a stomach ulcer out of *this* assignment, I mused, I never would. Soon the charade would begin.

Turning off the paved road onto a narrow dirt road, I began to wonder: How remote is this place? It's got to be an ideal place for a group of nudists, with no signs of life or other residences for miles.

Finally, a hand painted rustic sign that read "Resort" and an arrow pointing to a very narrow, winding, dusty road. Then another sign at a gate reading "Please Close Gate Behind You." Where was this adventure taking me? Yet another sign, "Slow Down, Prevent Dust" and about a quarter mile further, another sign, at last, indicating parking ahead. I rounded the corner and came upon a sea of cars parked in an open graveled field. I found a small space to park and then took a deep breath before stepping out of my now dust encrusted rental car.

As I looked around I noticed two naked men walking

up a small trail to what appeared to be a bath house. I was nervous and hoped I wouldn't embarrass myself by getting aroused by the sight of all these naked men. I had to admit, even though I was nervous, I felt a little tingle down below when I observed these first two naked men at this, my first, nudist experience.

I started to walk toward the sound of men's voices and laughter and then I stopped in awe as I looked over a hillside down onto a beautiful meadow nestled in the pine and oak trees along a peaceful small river. I took in a deep breath of clean fresh mountain air. The scent of the pine trees as they whispered in the air from the slight breeze was like a scene from a movie. Sort of a "*Brokeback Mountain*" experience. What a serene setting. And then I noticed about 40 or so naked men frolicking in the river and in the meadow or just soaking up the warm afternoon sun.

It looked like they were having a lot of fun and I was starting to warm up to the idea of being naked out here away from the rest of the world for a week. In fact, I had to remind myself I had a job to do and I was not here to necessarily have a good time. Although if I did enjoy it along the way, surely that would not be a bad thing.

Hiking down to the meadow from the parking lot, I was greeted by several of the men who offered their services to help me. I think the fact that I was fully clothed and they were all naked must have been somewhat erotic to them—like a Christmas present that needs to be unwrapped after all the others have been opened on Christmas Day.

A handsome, buffed man with blue gray eyes approached me. He was tall with a chiseled physique and it appeared he was Asian mixed with some other European background. "Welcome. Can I help you with something? Are you looking for George?"

"Ah, yes, thanks. I'm looking for George or Bruce."

"Sure thing. I think George is up at the cookhouse."

I couldn't help but stare at his muscular chest and confess I did venture a glance at his handsome hung cock. "OK, thanks. And where is the cookhouse?"

"Oh, sorry. Just up this trail, and look up to the large open-air gazebo which is the dining hall and cookhouse."

"Thanks."

"By the way, my name is James."

"Hey, thanks, James. I'm Tony. I'll head up there and see if George is around. Thanks again."

James seemed like a really nice and helpful individual. I did a double-take as I walked away to catch a rear view of James. As I walked up the path to the cookhouse, everything seemed strangely quiet, but it was already nearly three-thirty in the afternoon so the activity was all down below in the meadow.

As I came upon the open parking area near the cookhouse, still not seeing anyone around, I couldn't help but notice an old and very strange looking car that appeared to be something out of the Al Capone era. It was not pristine, but did appear to have been driven lately, so was obviously somebody's restoration project. Still looking around for some signs of life, I spotted an herb garden and the rounded yet muscular derriere of a naked man squatted in the garden pulling weeds. Maybe this was George.

"Hello, there." I yelled to him, hoping not to show any signs of shock or excitement once he stood and graced me with a full frontal shot of a naked man in hiking boots, sweating in the mid-day sun in the garden.

"Oh, Hello."

He was of medium build and somewhat hairy, masculine and middle aged, and quite attractive, I noticed right off. The beads of sweat on his hairy chest glistened in the sun. "Are you George?"

"No, George is up at the barn. I'm Bruce. Can I help you with something?"

"I hope so. I'm Tony. I'm here for the MANS event."

"Ah, yes, Tony. We were expecting you today. How was your flight from SoCal?"

"It was great; no problems. Sure is warm here, though...much more so than I remembered."

"Yeah, well, you'll enjoy getting out of those clothes and taking a dip in the river then."

I guess he believed that I was a true nudist, so that

was a good sign.

"You can settle up payment for the week with George later. Right now let me show you which yurt is yours."

We started back down the path I'd just come up, toward the campground area and the scattering of small cabin-like accommodations in front of us. "Yurt. . . That's a strange word. I've never heard of that before. What is a yurt actually?"

"Ha, yes! A yurt is a small structure usually made of canvass or very light construction.... Certainly not built to any code. You can see them down there in front of us."

"Wow, I didn't know that. It should be much better than actually tenting."

"Yes, very much so. You're in a double yurt all to yourself, so if you have a romantic rendezvous this week, you'll have some privacy. Many of the yurts are shared but we had sort of a cancellation, so it's all yours."

I took his lead and questioned him. "Cancellation?"

"Yeah. It's a long story but I'm sure you'll hear all the details about it soon from the rest of the guests. No need for me to go into that now."

"Here you go," he said. "Yurt number 8-A right off the river. The A is for Alderwood and I think you'll enjoy the sounds of the rushing river water—drowns out any other noises and the shrill sounds of the cicadas at night."

Listening to Bruce describe the location of my yurt, the one word that I focused on that made me cringe was "drowns." I couldn't help but think of Zack and the fact that he'd drowned right here at this very location on the river.

"By the way, what river is this? It's not very large."

"It is pretty small but in the winter months it can be mighty treacherous. This is the Cosumnes River. It runs through the entire length of our property. My partner and I have 311 acres here."

"Wow, how nice. That's a lot of land and a beautiful setting."

We started walking back toward the meadow so I could get my bags and I took this opportunity to enjoy the view walking behind Bruce as we trekked along the narrow footpath. His ass was muscular and slightly hairy, very sexy with his dark tan. "Yeah, George grew up on this land," he said, "and inherited the place when his parents passed on. It was run as a kids' camp for many years but then the insurance got to be too much, and they had to close it down."

"That's too bad. But at least the property is now being put to a good use."

"Actually, his parents were elderly at the time and ready to give it up. George loved growing up here and likes to regale guests of tales as a child. He'll want to take you on a hike to the swimming hole some time later in the week, you can be sure of that."

I was enjoying my chat with this sexy naked man and

was starting to find the whole thing erotic, and realized I had to suppress that feeling, if you get my drift. "So, how long have you and George been together?"

"Oh, gosh, it's been 16 years now."

"That's great. Sounds like a good match."

"Yeah, it's a pretty damn good life up here."

We reached the meadow just below the parking lot. "Well, thanks. I'll get the rest of my stuff.

"Great. Oh, and breakfast is at 8:30. Just listen for the chow bell. And lunch is at 12:30 and dinner at 7:00. You don't need to get dressed for meals, just bring a towel to sit on."

"Kewl, and I'll settle up with George later."

Bruce turned and started to head back to the cookhouse. "No problem. For now, just get naked and enjoy the week."

'*GULP*'

"Oh," he said, "do you need any help with your bags?"

"Oh, no, I didn't bring a lot...nudist, you know." Good one!

"OK, enjoy!"

I made one more trip back to my vehicle for a few things, taking my time just to avoid the inevitable. It didn't take long to get settled in. My yurt was located right near the shoreline which could have been how Zack wandered drunk to the edge of the river, slipped and hit his head. Even though his parents thought he no longer drank, he might have slipped up and decided to tie-one-on with his friends that first night around the campfire. That was actually pretty believable.

There are eight yurts located in Alderwood, and all of them no more than 25 to 50 feet apart, you'd think someone in the other yurts would have heard or seen something. But with the rushing sound of the river water, it's likely to have drowned out most any other sounds. I just needed to find out what it was that people knew about what happened that night.

Getting out of my clothes, I grabbed the sarong I brought as there was no way I was walking down that trail to the meadow struttin' my stuff bare-ass naked. And so now, it was show time.

I opened the flap to my yurt and stepped out into nature, (nearly) free of textiles...a liberating feeling...that is, until I see another individual.

# 5

## Naked in the Meadow

The walk down to the meadow seemed like miles considering all the thoughts that were now racing through my mind. Hopefully, I'd be able to deliver a believable performance as just another gay nudist guest for the week. I knew the gay part would not be a problem since I've been out and proud since about the age of twenty two—just shortly after graduating from college.

When I was in grade school I felt an attraction to other guys, but I felt this was probably normal, just part of the puberty thing. I remember having a huge crush on my eighth grade teacher. He was young and had the sexiest hairy arms and chest. I enjoyed getting a glimpse of his chest on the rare occasion that he'd wear an open collar polo shirt.

Then in high school, I had a part time job waiting tables at a small restaurant in Marin. The owner of the restaurant, who was also my boss, was openly gay. This was the first time I'd worked or socialized with an openly gay man, and I realized gays were no different than anyone else. That was when I started to think that I could be gay. I managed to remain in that closet until after college and some day I will tell you the story of how it was that I came out. I'm sure you'll enjoy that story.

Walking into the meadow, I noticed a cluster of naked men in the shade and a few scattered sun worshipers basking on towels and lawn chairs. Still others were enjoying some frolic in the refreshing waters of the river. Now the question was: Where should I gravitate since I didn't want to be perceived as unfriendly or anti-social?

I walked past a gazebo with a scattering of colorful ice chests of many shapes and sizes as well as a couple of large refrigerators. This appeared to be a social gathering area where the drinks were kept and the possible location of a happy hour. There were a few tables scattered here and there. Several guys were playing board games or cards and seemed to be very engrossed in their games, and I went pretty much unnoticed as I walked by.

One particular guest caught my eye and it wasn't because he was eye candy. This rather large man was planted at the edge of the meadow near the water in a large white Adirondack chair. Besides being quite large, he was very pale, and that combination on a naked man is not attractive. He looked like an ivory Buddha my aunt once had sitting on her fireplace mantle. As I walked past him, he looked up at me from the book he was reading and smiled and said hello. He seemed like a likeable person right from our first encounter. I found him somewhat curious, but doubted he would have anything to do with a possible murder. He was obviously not a very agile person. I couldn't see him having the opportunity to kill Zack or the temperament for such an act – and possibly he might have some information that could help me with my investigation—but still, I needed to check him out, along with any others who might have had a connection to Zack.

I continued on toward the bevy of naked men in the shade as this was more my style and would afford me the best opportunity to meet as many men as possible right off.

"Hey, mister. Welcome. My name's Cris."

Cris was a very slight framed, fair skinned man wearing a rather large brimmed coolie hat to keep the sun's rays off of his face.

"Oh, hi. I'm Tony."

Cris sprang to his knees to shake my hand and pointed out toward the water. "That hot man with the shaved head out in the water is my husband, Michael."

I wasn't sure which shaved headed man in the river he was referring to as there were several to pick from.

"Nice to meet you, Cris."

"You just arrived today?"

As I laid out my towel on the cool damp grass, I realized I'd need to disrobe next. "Yep, I just flew in this afternoon."

"Well, welcome. Where are you from?"

"San Diego." Ok, here goes. Off came the sarong and now I was naked in the meadow with everyone else. Suddenly, I was blending in just like a real nudist.

"Wow, San Diego? So, Tony, how did you hear about MANS and this week in Plymouth?"

Oops, I hadn't thought about that question. Neither Vinnie nor I had given that any thought.

Without missing much of a beat, though, and while fumbling in my backpack for my sunglasses, I responded, "Oh, a friend of mine, Blaine, told me about the event."

That was a good comeback and I was starting to get the hang of this charades thing. Good job.

"Oh, so you know Blaine from Portland?"

Maybe that hadn't been such a good comment to make after all. "Well...yes, but very casually."

"Do you also know Eric from Portland? He's here this week."

"No, I don't think I know him but I'm sure I'll meet him later. And Blaine wanted me to say hello for him too when I see him."

"Oh, I'm sorry, Tony. Let me introduce you to some of the other guys here. This is Frank. He's from Sacramento."

"Hey, Frank."

Frank's a very short, dark complexioned man, very Italian looking with a receding hair line. He seemed to be a pretty hyper individual. Could he have possibly lost his patience with Zack for some reason and maybe killed him accidentally? Who knows?

"And this is Russ, also from Sacramento. He rode up with us."

"Nice to meet you, Russ."

"Well, that remains to be seen now, doesn't it? Ha, ha."

Russ is a tall and attractive man with a slightly muscular, toned body. Nicely tanned all over with no tan lines and a very sexy hairy chest. Love those hairy-chested men. Russ is what I would refer to as an otter... hairy but not a bear. Russ reminded me of my last boyfriend. He even looked an awful lot like Brad, but his personality was much more flippant than Brad. I could see Russ having something to do with Zack's death, or perhaps knowing something.

Hell, at this point, in my mind any one of these guys could have killed Zack – if, in fact, I came to believe he *had* been murdered. I just needed to try and find a motive from any of them and then figure out how they might have killed him without leaving physical signs on his body.

Cris continued with introductions. "The two guys over there are from Santa Rosa. That's John and Jon."

"Hi, guys. A pair of Johns?"

Introductions done, Cris grabbed some sunscreen and began to coat his lily white chest, shoulders and arms. "We have a lot of Santa Rosa guys here this time as they always seem to enjoy the week with us Sacramento boys."

"Great! I'm sure I'll enjoy the week as well."

"So if you're from San Diego, you've probably been to the Malibu Gathering, CMEN?"

"Actually, I haven't. This is my first social nudity event...hmm, other than parties and beaches." Whew, good thinking! "What is Semen?"

"It's not what you're thinking. The event is actually C M E N, California Men Enjoying Nature, and it's a gay nudist gathering in Malibu at a resort there. It's actually a Jewish kids camp but the money they make in the off season by hosting the CMEN is too good for camp directors to pass up, and it works out well for the 300 or so men who attend."

"That sounds like a fun thing to do and Malibu is so close for me from San Diego. I could easily drive there. I'll have to keep that in mind."

"Yeah, do that...and check out their web site so you get a better idea of what's offered. It's a fun time."

Frank spoke up over Cris. "Tony, I think you'll enjoy our group too for this week. We're really nice guys, aren't we, Russ?"

Russ chose to ignore him.

Cris spotted James walking across the meadow. "Hey, James. Come over here a minute. I want you to meet someone."

"Oh, Cris, thanks. I already met James when I arrived."

James acknowledged me. "Hi, Tony. Did you find George after all?"

"I didn't find George, but ran into Bruce and he got me settled in."

"Great. Well, enjoy. I'm going to jump in that water—it looks refreshing."

And with that, James continued to stroll down to the water with all eyes adoring his well defined body and nice tan, not to mention the nice appendage between his legs that swung side to side as he walked.

Cris seemed to be very sociable and I was thinking that maybe this guy could help me a great deal with information. It was nice that we were positioned near each other so we could talk. But then again, even with his meek, but outgoing personality, he could be a murderer.

"So, Tony, I know you'll hear more about this during the week, but in case you notice an aura of somberness with the guys, it's because of an unfortunate accident that happened here the first night of the event. The guys have been pretty shook up about it."

To me, none of them seemed to be very shook up, with all the frolic in the river, Russ and Frank playing backgammon, and the other board games going on up at the gazebo. The fat man in the Adirondack was the only one who seemed to be somber, but I'd bet that was likely just his demeanor. And why was it that Cris would be the first to break out with the news of Zack's death. Was he trying to get something off his chest?

"So, Cris, what is it? What happened?" I tried to make it sound sincere that I had no clue as to what might have happened and I think it worked.

"Well, one of the guys drowned during the night swimming in the river."

"Oh my gawd. How terrible. So he died here?"

"Yep. There was a lot of excitement around here Friday morning and with all these naked men and the police and ambulance, and...."

"That's really terrible. How sad."

"Yeah. Zack was from Santa Rosa or somewhere near there. I think he lived in Guerneville actually."

"Wow. Did he have a partner or boyfriend here with him?"

"No, he was single. He came here with some friends from Santa Rosa, and his good friend Warren, who you'll meet later."

I was starting to get some good information and wanted to keep this conversation going. "That must have been awful. Who found him?"

"I'm not sure. Russ, did you ever hear who it was that found Zack?"

Russ looked up briefly from his backgammon game. "I heard it was John and Jon. They went down to the river early Friday morning to enjoy the sunrise over the mountains and some quiet time together. Guess they got more than they bargained for."

Just then, a blond fellow with a great tan walked up. "Hey...Eric, there you are. We missed you!"

"Hey, Cris,...guys." Eric had a deep sexy voice which added to the overall package.

"Yeah," said Cris. "I had to end up playing Frank in backgammon and I was looking forward to whipping your butt, you twerp!"

"Sorry, guys. Had to call my honey, and you know the only place to get a friggin' cellular signal here is up at the top of that hill. I hiked up there right after lunch. If I didn't call 'H,' I'd be paying for it when I got home."

"Well, at least you got in a cardio workout—that's a lot more than Michael and I've done—or most of the rest of the guys. Oh, Tony, did you meet Eric yet?"

"No, we haven't met—I would remember meeting him." I thought I'd flirt a little even though he had a boyfriend at home.

"Hi, Tony. Nice to meet you. Did you just get in today?"

"Yeah, I did and I have a message from Blaine. He said to tell you hello and he wishes he could be with us this week."

"Oh my gawd. So you know our little Bunny?"

That was a reference I had not heard before for Blaine, but I played along with it. "Yeah, I know him slightly.... Nice guy."

"Oh, yeah, Blaine is a sweetheart. Wish he could have made it this year. Well, guys, I'm going into the water— anyone care to join me?"

And with that, Eric was off to the water along with Russ and a couple of other guys. I realized there was a lot of information here I needed to glean and this was a good start. I needed to meet and get close to Warren as it seems he knew Zack better than most of the other guys from what I could tell. Warren also could have had some sort of unsettled grudge with Zack and that might have led him to murder.

"So, Cris, is that gazebo area sort of a meeting place or something?"

"Oh, yeah, Tony. We have a couple of happy hour cocktail parties up there. We had a welcome party there on Thursday, and this coming Tuesday night we'll have another cocktail party. It's also an area for guys to play board games or cards and just to hang out."

"If you have anything that needs to be refrigerated," he said, "you can put it in one of two up at the gazebo or you can leave an ice chest up there too if you have one. That's a nice area to just kick back and relax."

"Sort of like that...rather large guy up there in the chair does?"

"Oh, ha...you mean Tiny!"

"Tiny?"

"Yeah. Tiny's from Sacramento and is a very sweet guy—you'll love him. Very intelligent individual, too."

"Is that pretty much all he does all day?"

"Yeah, he doesn't get too physical. He's a diabetic and can't control his weight. He pretty much stays in that chair all day until he turns in for the night."

Tiny seemed like an interesting character. "Sorry to hear that, but I guess as long as he's doing what he likes and enjoying himself . . ."

"You got it, Tony. That's what this week is all about.... Well, here comes my husband!"

"Hey, babe," he yelled out. "Are you all shriveled from that water? You were in there long enough. Michael, I want you to meet Tony. He just arrived today."

Michael had a shaved head and seemed to be a very young at heart individual. He appeared to be in excellent shape, likely retired, and definitely older than Cris.

"Hey, Michael, nice to meet you!"

Michael extended his hand to shake mine. "Welcome, Tony! So where did you just get in from?"

"San Diego!"

"Great. Well, I'm sure you'll enjoy your week here. Who wouldn't, right?"

"Yeah!"

"*Ding, ding...ding, ding!*" There's the dinner bell.

Where did the afternoon go? Some progress was made today but I have my work cut out for me. I pulled my stuff together and wrapped my sarong around me, and like cows returning to the milk barn, we all headed up to the cookhouse on the hill—a place I was already familiar with, having my first encounter with Bruce up there.

My goal for this evening was to get to know Warren.

# 6

# Dining Al Fresco

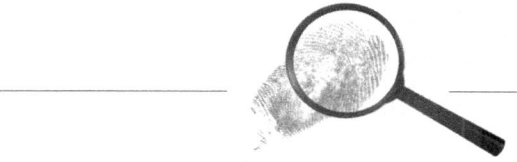

This was all such a new experience for me. Growing up as a child we certainly never had to dress for dinner but we always had to be dressed for dinner. Some of the guys arrived totally au naturel, while others—like me—showed a little more modesty, covering up with a sarong. I soon learned, though, that the sarongs came off and were used to cover the bench to sit on at the dining table. I, however, chose to keep mine tightly wrapped around me.

Waiting in the buffet line, the aroma of a good home cooked meal made me realize how hungry I was after a long day. Dinner was meatloaf, mashed potatoes and green beans. Mmm, a nice, good ol' home comfort food meal. Just as I completed the buffet line I heard my name called.

"Tony, over here!"

I wondered who this might be that was calling for

me and then I realized it was Cris. That was part of my comfort zone, so I gravitated toward Cris and Michael and their little group's table. I had hoped that possibly one of these men might be the ever elusive Warren that I had yet to meet.

"Hi, guys. Mind if I join you?"

"Sit! Tony, I think you know most everyone here?"

"Yeah,...That was fun today on the meadow. So what activities go on in the evening?"

I knew when I opened my mouth with that lead-in line around a group of gay men that I'd get some smart remark. Russ chimed in almost immediately.

"Well, Tony, there's always plenty of action in the hot tub if you're looking for that sort of thing. I'll meet you there at about ten o'clock tonight. <wink, wink>"

Cris shot Russ a dirty look and then commented, "Michael and I usually just hang out at the campfire and turn in early."

"That sounds really relaxing, and up here the stars are so bright and the air so clean and clear."

Michael spoke up, "Yeah, and Cris and I find we get up earlier up here than at home and there's coffee made and put out up here at 6:30."

"Eric, sit down and join us! Are you having any wine tonight?"

"Well, duh, of course!" said Eric with his hands on his hips giving Cris attitude.

"Eric, you met Tony today in the meadow, right?"

"I did, Cris. Thanks. Hi, Tony. Enjoying yourself?"

"I am. Seems like a nice group of guys."

"Eric, did you know that Tony knows your good friend Blaine from Portland?"

"Anyone want some wine?...So I hear...what a small world! How was it again that you know Blaine, Tony?"

Oh boy, here we go! "I really don't know him well; he's just an acquaintance I made in San Diego since he's been going there lately for his work."

"Work?" Eric's voice now raised. "You call that work—doing something fun that you enjoy?"

I spoke up in defense of Blaine. "Well, I guess for him it is, since he has to sell himself and his artistic ability to make a living."

Russ spoke out, "Yeah, sort of like we do every day at our jobs—sell ourselves and our abilities."

That was a good point that Russ made.

There was something about Russ that seemed a little different. He came off as impersonal and flippant about most things. But yet there seemed to be a soft side to him as well that people might not see right off. Could he be a possible suspect for murder? Actually, from my standpoint, all forty-two guys including the resort owners were suspects. I needed to get Cris off on his own and see if I could find out a little more about Russ, and also find a way to meet Warren.

"So, Cris, you said there are a lot of guys from Santa Rosa here this week?"

"Yeah, there are...Frank, how many guys are from the Santa Rosa group or that area this week?"

"I think there were fifteen booked from Santa Rosa the last time I checked with Paul. Of course that included Zack, poor guy."

"And Cris, you mentioned Warren, from Santa Rosa. Is he close by? I'd like to meet him."

Cris immediately began to scan the crowd of men to point out Warren.

"You'll like Warren, and he's single too. Nice guy, so sweet. Oh there he is...the table nearest the entrance over there. He's the guy on the far side facing us on the end."

I turned to focus on the table that Cris was speaking of. "Oh, OK...the end by the entrance or the end by the rail?"

"By the rail—the stocky guy with the shaved head and the adorable smile."

"Oh, yes, he does have a great smile. I'll have to introduce myself to him when I get a chance."

We continued to banter back and forth all through dinner, with a lot of laughs and good natured ribbing. Still, there was something about Russ that just did not sit well with me, but I couldn't quite figure out what it was that bothered me.

"So, Russ...you're from Sacramento, I take it, and part

of the MANS group?"

"Yes!"

Frank had to chuckle at that response. "But he never does anything with the group unless it's the Rancho Sierra weekend or something else that's fun!"

"Oh, shut up, Frank. I do, too. It's just I'm a very busy man, you know, and I have a life outside of MANS."

"Yeah, Russ has a life on **gay.com!**"

"Well, Michael, it's better than cruising a bath house."

"Hmm!" Michael bit his tongue and had no response to that comment.

I wanted to talk to Eric too after dinner. "So Eric, are you planning to hang out at the campfire after dinner as well?"

"Yeah, pretty much everyone does or they sit in the hot tub—one or the other. If it's warm enough this evening we could get a competitive card game going up here like we did the first night."

I picked up on what Eric had said about the card game and that being the first night, Thursday, the night Zack died. "So you guys had a fun time playing cards on Thursday evening?"

"It was a lot of good fun. We must have played until midnight or later."

"So, who are the card players here? I enjoy cards sometimes. Who was playing that night?"

"Oh, gosh! Russ was there. Cris and Mike were there.

Some of the Santa Rosa guys that I met that night for the first time hung around for a while. It's a lot of fun and some good natured players. Well...except for Russ." He whispered to me. "He gets a little competitive."

Just before we finished dinner, George stood up to welcome everyone, and lay down a few house rules of the resort. It was nice to put a face with his name since I'd already met Bruce when I arrived.

George is a tall stocky man with salt and pepper hair and of course a deep dark all-over tan. The hair pattern on his chest ran down the front of his belly like a pathway to paradise down below. George was well hung and not at all shy about his body. Once George was done with his little speech, I immediately went up to him and introduced myself and told him I'd settle up payment with him later.

The guys cleared the table and dishes, and one by one began to wander off only to reconvene later by the campfire. There was a chill in the air now and I knew I'd need a light sweatshirt this evening. The thought of a campfire sounded nice actually...reminiscent of middle school summer camp where we sat around a campfire singing *Kum bah yah* and made s'mores.

"See you guys later!" Eric called out as I walked off with Cris and Michael to head back to Alderwood. The plan was to lather bug spray on our naked bodies and to fetch a flashlight for the trail hike back late at night. I was warned of the rattlesnakes in the area and that was the last thing I wanted to encounter.

We sat at a picnic table for a while in Alderwood, just Cris and Michael and me. Michael was preoccupied stuffing a glass pipe in preparations for a few hits before heading up to the campfire. It appeared that Cris would join him, but I hadn't smoked since I was in college. That would be just what I needed to blow my cover in the investigation.

"Here you go, Cris."

"Thanks, babe. *Shhhoooop!*...Tony, want a hit?"

"Oh, no thanks. I don't smoke any more...allergies!"

"So have you two known Russ for a long time?"

"Oh, yeah...long, long time." Cris said, and it seemed as if he was responding with a double meaning and hoping I would read between the lines.

"Is that a bad thing? The way you say it makes me wonder. He seems to be very flippant and insincere. Does he have a boyfriend?"

"Oh, he's a nice enough person. Sometimes he tries too hard. He's had lots of bf's in the past. He tried to have a week long affair here but the guy went and died on him."

Cris chided, "Michael, that's not a very nice thing to say."

"Well, it's true."

This was an interesting comment. "Really, what do you mean? Were he and Zack a couple or something?"

"I think Russ had hoped to hook up with him, but from what I overheard in the showers, it was not going to happen."

"Michael, you shouldn't talk like that!"

"I'm just telling Tony what I know and what I heard."

"What exactly did you hear, Michael?"

"Well, this had to have been the first night we were here as that was the only night Zack spent here before... you know."

"Really?"

"Yeah, a bunch of us were in the hot tub and Russ was playing footsies with Zack. Finally Zack got out of the hot tub and headed for the showers."

"So Zack shut Russ down with his advances?"

"Well, it was only a few minutes later I went up to the showers to brush my teeth and join Cris already in bed, and I caught Russ and Zack both in a shower stall together. From the conversation, I think Russ moved in on him in the showers and Zack was not pleased."

Could this be the motive for Zack's death? "That would upset me too if the advance was not welcomed," I said.

Michael started to put his paraphernalia away now. "Then their voices were no longer whispers and finally I heard Zack say something to the effect of 'I can't do that. It would just ruin everything. Just leave me alone!'"

"Wow!"

"Then Zack bolted from the shower stall and with a startled 'deer in the headlights' look at seeing me there, he quickly wrapped himself in a towel and left the showers."

"And it was that night that he died?"

"Yeah. Pretty ironic, hey?"

"What do you think Zack meant when he said 'that would ruin everything?'"

"I'm not sure. What do you think, Cris?"

"I don't know, Michael. Possibly Warren might know. I know he's pretty close...or *was* pretty close to Zack."

"Yeah, I know most of those guys are all part of LIAHO, the nudist group from Santa Rosa, so I'm sure they all know more about Zack than either Cris or I would."

"Why are you so curious about all of this anyway?" Cris asked.

Yikes, I hoped I wasn't sounding too suspicious to them with all these questions. I had to think fast.... "Oh, no reason. I'm just a curious person, I guess. I'm fascinated with forensics and took some classes in school in that sort of thing."

A voice from the darkened trail pierced the night air. "Hey guys, are you headed up to the campfire?"

"Sure, Eric. Is it burning yet?"

"Oh, yeah, and the guys are gathering around. Dan brought out his mandolin to play and I'm sure there'll be some campfire songs breaking out soon."

"Well, let's go, guys!"

And so we grabbed our flashlights and sweatshirts and headed out to join the rest of the guys for an evening by the campfire.

# 7

# Rally 'Round the Campfire

As I approached the glow of the campfire and the sounds of a lone mandolin playing, the mood seemed to be, for the first time, somber. Maybe the guys were reflecting on the events that took place earlier in the week with the demise of Zack or maybe they were all just coming down from an active day of play in the sun.

The grey smoke from the fire was trailing straight up into the black night sky toward the twinkling stars scattered in the universe. The piercing sound of the cicada in the air nearly drowned out the rush of the river water over the rocks. It was so serene and peaceful.

Cris, Michael and Eric stopped off at the hot tub while I continued on to the campfire. I surveyed the crowd, and realized there was a stack of resin chairs to pick from and then determine where the best location would be to help me learn more about Zack. Fortunately for me, there was an open space just one seat away from

Warren. This would help me to get to know him better and learn more about his relationship to Zack.

"Hey, guys, mind if I move in here?"

"Not at all. Pull up your chair.... My name's Art and this is Warren."

"Hi, Art...Warren. I'm Tony."

"We noticed you arrive today. I had to wake up Warren who was napping in the hammock in the meadow to point out the new kid."

I found that comment complimentary. "Ha, ha...seems like the last to arrive is always the most ambiguous, right?"

"Well, I would assume you're here filling the reservation that was vacated by Zack, right?"

"That's what I understand, Warren. I was unaware of any drama or anything that took place, until I arrived."

"With Zack there was always a lot of drama...right, Art?"

"Well, somewhat, but you know how it is when you're that age and you're as good looking as Zack was."

There was a pause in the conversation, but I wanted to keep the line of questioning going. "So you guys knew Zack pretty well?"

"He was in our nudist group and I used to see him at most of the house parties and pool parties for LIAHO. Warren knew him better, having socialized with him outside the group."

"Really? So why do you say there was a lot of drama

surrounding Zack, Warren?"

"Oh, it's no big deal. It seems that Zack was always being singled out as a victim and always feeling sorry for himself. I loved him dearly, but he was a little bit high maintenance, if you know what I mean."

"Yeah, some guys are like that...seems like a lot of work to be their friend. And why do we put up with a friendship like that?"

"There was something about Zack that I felt he needed me for. Maybe I was like a big brother or mentor to him, but I know he appreciated all the advice I gave him at his times of need." Warren's voice was starting to break up as he became somewhat emotional thinking of Zack.

Maybe Zack no longer felt he needed support from Warren and the thought of losing his friendship was overwhelming for Warren. Could he have chosen to eliminate Zack rather than lose him as his understudy and good friend?

I am usually a pretty good judge of character. I didn't really think Warren was capable of murder from what I observed. He seemed to be sincere in his friendship and likely would not even step on a bug if he could avoid it.

"Can we talk about something else, guys?" Art spoke up. "I'm on vacation and I don't want to dwell on doom and gloom."

"Sure thing, Art. Sorry!...So what sorts of activities

are planned for the week?"

Art seemed to be very uncomfortable speaking of Zack. Could he have something to do with his murder? Could he have been jealous of the friendship between Zack and Warren and want more time with Warren?

Warren grabbed another log for the fire. "Well, you can be sure George will lead a hike up to the ol' swimming hole. He loves doing that and pointing out the flora and fauna along the way."

"AND...the rattlesnakes! George grew up on this property so he knows it really well and is very comfortable with the rattlesnakes up here."

I shuddered. "Yuk, I hate snakes, and especially rattlesnakes!"

"Well, just be careful when hiking on the rocks and be sure to use a flashlight when headed back up to Alderwood to the yurts."

"Thanks, Warren. I'll keep that in mind."

Someone had brought a bag of marshmallows and the guys were passing them around to skewer on the end of sticks and roast over the open fire. All we needed was some chocolate candy and graham crackers to make s'mores and life would be perfect here at Rancho Sierra.

With just the smell of burning Alderwood and Oak, the air was suddenly permeated by the scent of Patchouli oil. Who was that wearing that strong sweet smelling scent? It was very obnoxious and I was not the only one who noticed it. But then the scent was gone almost as quickly as it had come.

I wanted to get back to our conversation. "So is your LIA...LI.. ."

"LIAHO!"

". . . your LIAHO group pretty active with parties and such?"

Art spoke up. "We try to have at least one house or pool party a month at someone's house. Then during the summer we have other events planned like this week here."

"Great. Sounds like it's a pretty close group."

Art seemed to want to talk more about the group and was on the edge of his seat now. "Yeah, I just had a party at my house last week."

"That was a fun party, Art!"

"It was, until the spat with Zack and James. Then I think most of the guys just wanted to call it a night and get the hell out of there. I wish James and Zack would have kept that to themselves. It made people feel very uncomfortable that night."

Hmm, this was the first time I'd heard Zack's name mentioned in connection with James. "Zack and who?"

"Hey, guys! Mind if I join you?"

"Not at all, Paul. You need to take a break. It's been a little stressful for you."

"Gawd, I'll say it has.... Hi, I'm Paul; you must be

Tony? I heard you had checked in this afternoon and I noticed you at dinner."

"Nice to meet you, Paul. So you organized this event for MANS?"

"Yeah, pretty much—with some help from some of the other guys too. Frank is a lifesaver and Cris and Michael are a big help too."

"You need help with an event of this size, I'm sure." I had some experience with group organizations myself back in my college days. I served as Sentinel for our Business Club on campus and with my artistic abilities, I always got *volunteered* to head up decorating committees for parties and banquets.

"It's not bad; George and Bruce are so easy to work with. I take it you met them already?"

"Oh, yeah...seem like nice guys—and handsome, too."

"Oh, they are, but George will talk your ear off, especially if you get him on a discussion of old cars."

"I did notice some old car parked up by the cookhouse."

"Oh, that's his pride and joy. He's been working on restoring that one for years now."

"What is it, anyway?...very strange looking."

With one hand on his hip, Paul responded. "That, my dear, is a 1939 Hupmobile."

I had never heard of that. "A what?"

"Hupmobile! Hupmobile Skylark—only 319 ever made. That is George's baby."

"It sure seemed to be in great shape for as old as it is. 1939? Wow!"

"George has some other cars up at the barn and if you're interested, just ask him and he'll be glad to take you on a tour."

"Thanks. That's interesting."

I had wanted to find out more about the comment that Art made about Zack at his party and the apparent argument he'd had but I couldn't get back on the conversation without being too obvious. Besides, Art had made it clear he didn't care to discuss any of that now and wanted to enjoy a relaxing evening around the campfire.

"Hey, Russ, you're going to wet the bed if you keep playing with that fire! Didn't your mama tell you that?" someone said, while Russ was stoking the fire and adding more wood. It seemed to be burning plenty hot as it was.

"Who's sleeping with Russ tonight? He's going to wet the bed—just a warning!"

"Oh, shut up—somebody has to keep the fire going."

After about an hour at the campfire, I decided maybe I should turn in and collect the thoughts I had for the day to see if any of it was starting to make sense. Hopefully tomorrow would be a more productive day as I began to piece more details together.

I said my goodnights to the group and as I headed toward the meadow in the shadows, I noticed the mysterious Tiny was still seated in the same chair he'd been in when I arrived. He seemed to just sit there and observe the happenings of the day. This could be a good person to talk to. Perhaps tomorrow I'd pull up a chair next to him and see what I could learn from him. I'm sure he'd be a great source and judge of character.

The narrow path back to my yurt was dark and I was glad I had my flashlight. As I approached my yurt the thought of crawling into my bed was sounding mighty good to me now after a long day. I slipped between the sheets, taking a deep breath of the fresh mountain air and listening to the rush of the water over the river rocks. It was all so restful. My intentions had been to gather my thoughts together, but I knew it wouldn't be long before I would be sound asleep. And...I was!

# 8

# Dawning of a New Day

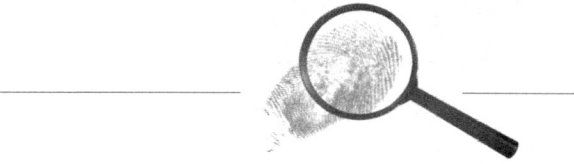

The sun seemed to rise earlier here, or maybe it was the great outdoors, the scent of the pine trees, the sounds of the wilderness critters or the river water rushing over the rocks that made me want to get up and start the day. I peeked out my yurt door and the warm glow of the sun was so inviting. I couldn't resist stumbling out of my yurt buck naked and headed for the warm rocks like a lizard soaking up the sun. The only thing that would make it any better would be to have a cup of coffee in my hand. I recall someone saying coffee was put out early up at the cookhouse, but I was hoping maybe for a yurt delivery service. NOT!

No one else was up yet, so I was not shy to be naked, even with my morning semi-pudgy I was still sporting. That would be gone soon. I felt very comfortable being au naturel this morning and was surprised to realize that some of my inhibitions were definitely slipping away. I perched myself upon a partially submerged rock on the river's edge in the sun and tried to gather my thoughts for today's adventure.

After about twenty minutes of meditation and still no one else stirring in Alderwood campgrounds, I decided I really needed that first cup of coffee. So I grabbed my sarong and hiked up to the cookhouse. There was little activity at this time of the morning, but as I passed the meadow, I noticed Tiny was already seated in his chair, much like I had left him last night in the shadows. He was reading a book and enjoying the early morning quiet. That was about to change as my intention was to get that first cup of coffee and then join him to see what I could find out about the other guests—and especially anything about Zack that might be helpful.

Reaching the top of the path to the cookhouse, I came across another guest that I had not met yet. This was a rather tall lean young man with a nicely toned body, and a full head of closely cropped sandy brown hair.

"Hey, morning! I'm Tony!"

He extended his hand to me. "Morning, Tony. Jake."

"Looks like there are only a handful of us up at this time of the morning."

"Yeah, I usually like to get up early and get my day going. Are you going to join us in the meadow later for naked yoga?"

Hmm, the visual in my mind of naked yoga made me

nearly visibly shudder. "I didn't know there was a yoga class this morning. I enjoy yoga classes at my gym but have never taken a naked yoga class before."

"Well, you'll have to join us later. I'm the instructor so I won't be too hard on you, I promise."

I tried to imagine being stark bare-ass naked doing some of those poses for yoga and the thought of being spread eagle in front of another row of naked yoga men was something I was just not that comfortable with. "Maybe!...I'll see about doing that, but don't count on it and don't wait up for me. Ha!"

"Well, OK. But Tony, you have a nice compact muscular body and I'd like to help you stretch those muscles." Jake's hand was now resting on my shoulder giving me a slight massage, and I was feeling a tent starting to form under my sarong.

"Thanks, Jake. I would enjoy watching you instructing us and will check it out later. You have a really nice tight body." I didn't know what else to say and if I carried on too much longer, I would surely embarrass myself. He was a very sexy man and I lusted at the thought of kissing those full lips.

"OK, it's a date, Tony! And maybe later I can give you a full body massage in the meadow. You probably need to be pampered a little. What d'ya say?"

The thought of his hands caressing my naked body had me fully aroused now. "It sounds good and I might have to take you up on that or take a rain check."

Jake winked at me and he walked off. My erection now starting to subside, I headed back to the meadow where I had seen Tiny.

It was obvious that Tiny didn't hear me approaching. "Morning!"

"Oh, good morning! I didn't see you coming up."

"Sorry to startle you. It's so nice at this time of the morning." I had my coffee now so life was good.

"Yes, it is. Love to kick back and relax with a good book."

"What are you reading?"

"'*Audacity of Hope*'—it's really good!"

"I haven't read it yet, but I'm sure I will eventually.... So I understand they call you Tiny?"

"Ha, ha. Yes, that's my nickname for obvious reasons. My real name is Chuck, or Charles if you want to be totally formal. And if I recall hearing from the others, your name is Tony?"

"Yes, 'tis I, Tony. I see you enjoy just watching people, and I'll bet you observe a lot during the day."

"Oh, yes...and the night time too. You'd be surprised."

"I like observing people too. Anything fun or interesting happen thus far in the week?"

"Well, I guess if you call the death of one of the guests 'interesting,' that could be considered something."

"Oh, yeah...that. Was there anything interesting in connection with Zack before they found him in the river?"

"The thing that I found odd is that the police said he was drunk and slipped in the river and hit his head."

Trying now not to seem too anxious, I said, "...So why was that odd to you?"

"Well...Zack didn't drink. I had watched the guys all that day and at the cocktail party and even after dinner, and I never once saw Zack take a drink."

"Do you think it could have been drugs and not alcohol?"

"No, I don't think so. Zack didn't seem like the type to me. He was a good kid from what I could tell."

"Wow, that does seem strange."

"Yeah, I thought so. I'm telling you, I see a lot of things going on because I spend a lot of time observing people. People don't talk that much to me because of my size. They might say 'Hello' to me but they don't stick around me so that gives me a lot of time to just observe people—which I love to do."

"I enjoy that too. Sorry the guys don't spend more time with you, but I know from what I've heard, the Sacramento group all thinks the world of you. I've heard them more than once already with some complimentary comments about you."

"That's nice to hear, and I thought maybe I had a good relationship with most of them. It's just they want to be around someone who's more active than I am and also someone who offers more eye candy for them."

Tiny shifted in his seat like he was beginning to

feel uncomfortable with all my questioning...or maybe there was something that bothered him. "You know, Tony, I recall the night that Zack died, I was sitting here in this chair and it was very dark here in the meadow, as there was only a sliver of a moon that night. I recall a very strange sweet smell that night but yet I didn't see anyone or even hear anyone. It was almost like a spirit had moved through here."

"Really?...strange."

"Do you believe in spirits or ghosts, Tony?"

"Let's put it this way. I've had no experience with that and have not given it much thought. Do you think the smell you recall was possibly a cologne, or maybe Patchouli?"

"You know, now that you say that, it could have been Patchouli scent – I've not smelled that since my college days."

"Same here...but I did smell someone wearing the oil just last night around the campfire, but I couldn't figure out who it was."

With a puzzled look, Tiny replied, "I didn't notice that last night and I was out here all evening."

"Tiny, was there any arguing or fights prior to the discovery of Zack's body Friday morning?"

"Do you always ask so many questions? I feel like I'm being interrogated."

It seemed as though I was starting to piss Tiny off somewhat with all my questions. "Sorry, it's just that this whole thing with Zack is sounding more and more weird all the time, and I find all of this stuff fascinating."

"Sounds like you should be a detective, Tony! You missed your calling. By the way, what sort of work do you do in San Diego? It is San Diego, isn't it?"

"Yes." I had not given the possibility of that question any thought and had to think fast. "Well, right now, I'm not employed, but I was working tending bar at Moe's in the Hillcrest in San Diego. They just laid off a couple of us guys since business has slowed with the economy and all."

"Seems to be something going around lately!"

"So, how about it?...Do you recall any arguments involving Zack before he turned up dead in the river?"

"You have a way with words, Mr. Tony! The only arguments I recall seemed to be something on-going and so were not out of the ordinary.... Seems like Zack and James were always at each other, and I'm not sure if that was part of a love fest or actual disdain for one another."

"Really?"

"And of course Zack and Russ had a little thing too, but that was short lived. That romance was squelched before it had a chance to blossom."

"So I hear. I wonder why that was."

"Like I say, Zack seemed to be obsessed with James."

"Now, I know I've met James, but what does he look like again? Refresh my memory."

"James is the good looking, buffed oriental stud. I

know that sounds like an oxymoron, buffed and Asian, but he is. I think he's not all Asian, and he does work out – that's obvious."

"Ah, yes. Now I recall James—the one with the really kewl eyes. I think someone said he's with a guy named Cameron for this trip?"

"Yes, Cam is his bf from the City, but I'm not sure how Zack fits into the equation."

Just about that time, Eric walked up with a cup of coffee. "Mornin' men! Looks like there are only a handful of us up at this time of day. Can I join you for a bit?"

I was very pleased with the information I'd managed to get from Tiny and chances are if I'd gone on too much longer, he might have become suspicious of me, so Eric's timing was actually perfect. "Morning, Eric." I said. "Please do pull up a chair and join us. So what did you end up doing last night?"

Tiny had a quick comeback. "Maybe you should ask him *who* he ended up doing last night!"

I jumped in with my thoughts. "I take it you observed something I didn't, Tiny?"

"Now, guys, don't let your imaginations get too carried away," grinned Eric like a Cheshire Cat. "I just walked back to the camp with Cris and Mike and went to bed all by myself. I've got a husband at home, don't forget."

**"Ding, ding...ding, ding!"** "There it is—breakfast

time!"

"Is it that time already? Looks like a lot of people are going to skip breakfast this morning."

"Oh, you'll be surprised, Tony; the bell brings them all out of their hole."

Eric and I walked up to the cookhouse together, buck naked all the way, as by this time I was feeling very comfortable in my own skin. My sarong over my shoulder was just for sitting on, as was the case with most of the guys.

The breakfast buffet looked to be a hearty meal but, not being all that much into breakfast, I grabbed a toasted bagel and some cream cheese along with a couple of bacon slices. I noticed Warren sitting by himself, so I joined him with hopes of finding out more about the LIAHO party he spoke of earlier before Art silenced him.

"Hey, Warren. Morning!"

"Morning, Tony! Save some space for a couple of the LIAHO guys that are coming up."

Spreading out my sarong on the bench, "Will do. How was your evening?"

"It was good – relaxing—and that is always good! How was your first night, Tony?"

"Great. I slept like a baby with the sounds of that river water rushing over the rocks."

"Glad to hear it."

"Warren, I was surprised at Art's response yesterday

when you started to talk about Zack at Art's party."

"Oh, that...well, Art is really good about not saying anything negative about anyone and since Zack is no longer with us, I think he was even more sensitive to that."

"So what did happen at the LIAHO party that caused people to leave the party?"

"Oh it was no big deal. Zack and James got into another one of their fights. It happened a lot with those two."

"Really?"

"This time was a little different since this was the first time that James had brought Cam to a party, and I think it really made Zack jealous."

"So did James and Zack date before Cameron?"

"Zack and James were in a relationship for eight years and most of those were pretty good years from what Zack always told me."

"Wow, I didn't realize that. I wonder what ended it for them."

"James ended it when he started screwing around with a younger, hot man. He was over Zack and wanted someone younger to make *him* feel younger and more desirable. You know that mid-life crises thing, I guess."

"That's too bad."

"Yeah, and I guess Zack was asking James for his share of the stuff they had, and James was being an asshole about it all, so Zack told him he would get an attorney to sue his ass and get a palimony settlement."

"I'll bet that didn't go over well! Yikes!"

"Ohh, no! James is not the type to be threatened. He was concerned about his job too, with a palimony suit."

"What sort of work does James do?"

"He's a pharmaceutical rep for one of the major drug companies—not sure which one."

"Morning, men!" Our conversation was interrupted by Art and another of the LIAHO guys. There goes *that* conversation—and just when it was getting good, too.

"Morning, Art,...Roger! Roger, did you meet Tony yesterday?"

"No, I don't think I did. Pleased to meet you, Tony. You have the sexiest dark eyes—you must be Italian!"

"Oh, thanks – they're just plain ol' brown, and yes I am Italian as a matter of fact."

About that time Paul walked up to join us. "Good morning, Paul."

"Hey, guys!"

"So, everything going well with the event planning? Are you off duty now?"

"Going good aside from a few glitches earlier that we worked out. All is going well now. We had a slight problem in communication about the special meals."

"So what happened?" Roger spoke up and I was glad he did, because I was curious too.

"Oh, you know we always have a couple of vegetarian guests and some Jewish guys who can't eat pork, but this year we had two diabetic guests. Or, we did have two. Bruce forgot to plan special meals for them but now that Zack is gone, Tiny is the only one left and his condition's not so serious that he has to worry all that much."

So now, was it possible that Zack might have had problems with his sugar levels because of what he was eating and that caused him to pass out in the river and drown? If only there had been an autopsy on the body, some of these questions might have been cleared up.

Trying to make conversation, I spoke up. "Wow, you don't realize how much goes into planning an event like this. I never thought about that."

"It's a lot of work but well worth it when it all comes together," said Paul. "I just love this event each year. So glad that Geno worked out the details for our group to come up here long ago, and glad too that he put so much of himself into forming the MANS group originally."

"Who's that, Paul?" I asked.

"Oh, Geno? He's not here this year, but he was one of the founders and original President of the MANS group a few years ago."

Warren had just returned to the table with a second glass of orange juice and caught the tale end of our conversation. "So where's Geno now, Paul? How come he's not here this year?"

"Geno retired and moved to Palm Springs last year. Enjoying life in the desert sun."

"So he's down in my part of the state, eh?"

"Sort of, Tony," said Warren. "I guess San Diego is not all that far from Palm Springs."

"Geno's probably enjoying the White Party this week." I couldn't help but throw that out because that should have been *me* this week.

"Well, guys, I'm headed down to the meadow to soak up some sun before it gets too much hotter. Anyone up for a game of backgammon later?"

"Wait up, Warren. I'll walk down with you. I'm finished too."

"OK, Tony, but you need to challenge me in backgammon!"

"You're on, Warren!"

# 9

## Naked Croquet, Anyone?

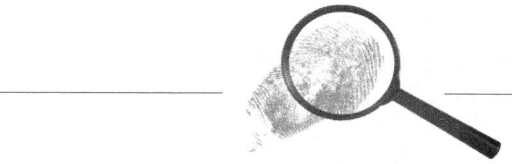

Walking back to the meadow with Warren, I knew this would be an ideal time to get him back on the discussion of Zack again, without anyone else being around to interrupt us. The problem was how to do that discretely without being too obvious.

"It's nice that James isn't letting this whole thing upset him, and he and Cameron can still enjoy the week. I should think that would be pretty hard on him too."

"Yeah, I guess!"

"Well, after all those years together, there must be a certain bond between two individuals and I'd think it's pretty emotional to know Zack is gone."

"I don't think James looked at it as if there was any sort of bond between them," he said. "More like a 'thorn in his side,' if anything."

"That's too bad!"

"I kept telling Zack to just move on with his life and

let it go, but he couldn't. He always thought they'd get back together."

"So it was James who broke it off with Zack?"

"As I said before, he dumped him for a younger man—Cameron."

"Ouch, that does hurt...been there before."

"I think it's sort of a mid-life crisis thing with James, but he always did like surrounding himself with the younger pretty boys. That's what attracted him to Zack originally."

"Funny how beauty tends to fade with age and sometimes the love fades too."

I wanted to find out more about the relationship between Warren and Zack. "Did you and Zack ever fight over this love he continued to have for James?"

"Who? Zack and I? No way! He trusted me and I was always there for him no matter what. We had a good friendship.... I miss him."

Once we got back to the meadow I noticed a group had already started to form in anticipation of the yoga class. "Hey, Tony, you going to join us for yoga?"

"No, Russ, I don't think I will."

"Oh, c'mon...you ever taken a yoga class before?"

"Oh, yes, I take classes back home, but never a naked class."

"It'll be fun; you can stand right in front of me!"

Just then Jake walked up to the group and strangely

enough I could once again smell the scent of Patchouli. "So are you guys all ready to do some stretching this morning?"

Now why was it that Jake had that scent about him? Was he the phantom that Tiny smelled moving through the meadow the night Zack died? Could he have had something to do with his death?

"Ok, guys, let's spread out a towel and get started. Tony, sexy man, you going to join us or are you just a voyeur?"

With that comment I decided I would fall into formation and do the class. I was really hoping to find out more about this mysterious scent and this would allow me to get to know Jake a little better.

Maybe if I could find out more about Jake, I could hopefully rule him out as a suspect in Zack's death. He was just too handsome to be guilty of such a thing, right? However, that mysterious scent had me wondering about him and what went on the night Zack died.

Russ had lined up directly in front of me and every time he contorted his body I was looking right at his sexy ass and those low-hanging balls in my face. It was quite surprising that I didn't get aroused by this, but I truly was getting comfortable with the nudity thing.

Jake was walking through the group helping the guys stretch properly and he seemed to focus on me a lot. Not sure if I was that bad with my form, or he just liked placing his hands on my body. I was not complaining, however.

The stretching and breathing felt very rejuvenating

and after 40 minutes of that, we all just laid on our towels for a few minutes. "Gawd, that felt so good!" I heard Russ finally speak.

"That was great. I needed that."

Jake started to walk over to me. "You did very well, Tony!"

"I'm glad you think so. I feel better – that's for sure."

"Wait until you have one of my massages."

Bingo! I realized that was likely the scent I had smelled. "Did you give a massage this morning, Jake?"

"Yeah, can you smell the oils on me?"

"I can and I was wondering what that sweet smell was."

"Sorry...that's massage oil I use that has Patchouli oil in it. Some guys love it but others can't stand the smell."

"Well, it's very distinctive."

"We don't need to use that one when I work you over."

So now I needed to figure out who had a massage from Jake Thursday night—the night Zack died—and that could reveal the identity of this mysterious phantom that Tiny recalled. Or could it have been Jake himself?

Is it possible that Zack and Jake had some interaction? Did Jake know Zack before meeting him here at Rancho Sierra?

"So, Jake, is there a sign-up sheet for your massages?"

"Yeah, up on the corkboard at the cookhouse, but you don't need to sign up, I'll massage you any time you're ready."

"Thanks, I'll keep that in mind—and thanks for the yoga class. That was a new experience for me. Naked yoga!"

"Say, Jake, did you give Zack a message when he arrived on Thursday?"

"Who?"

"Zack, the young man who drowned."

"No, I really don't recall having met him. I didn't arrive until late in the evening on Thursday."

As I walked away to join the other guys in the meadow, I knew I had to check out the massage sign-up sheet. I was hoping that the prior day's sign-up sheet was still posted. I walked up toward the bathhouse like I was headed to use the john, and continued on over to the cookhouse.

Since we were between meals, the cookhouse was totally quiet with no one around. Checking out the corkboard that I hadn't even noticed before, I located the massage sign-up sheet. "Jake, Hands of Pleasure, Sign Up"—and fortunately the prior days' names were all there.

Looking back at Thursday's sheet, Jake had one late afternoon massage and one night massage. That was strange since Jake said he hadn't gotten in until late evening on Thursday.

At 8:45 p.m. he massaged Cameron. Before that he had a massage scheduled with Art at 3:30—so he was definitely here before late evening as he had told me.

Why would he have lied to me about that—perhaps he was trying to come up with an alibi?

I thought I'd better head back down to the meadow before anyone became curious about my whereabouts. I wanted to try and talk some more with Warren and, if I recalled, we still had a backgammon challenge to play out.

"Hey, Warren...so, are you up for that game of backgammon?"

"There you are. I thought maybe you chickened out on me."

"Sure, I'm ready...Warren, do you want the brown or the white men?"

"I like my men brown and tanned all over!"

As we continued with our game of backgammon and making small talk, my mind kept rehashing all the details I'd managed to glean about Zack and James. I felt James was pretty nonchalant about Zack's death and that was weird to me. Could he have had something to do with his death? From what I was hearing there was no love lost.

However, Cameron could have been jealous of Zack and may have had reason to kill him.

Then again, something was strange about Jake. Why did he lie about Thursday evening? Was he also lying about knowing Zack?

And Russ—could he have been upset enough with

Zack to get into a fight with him that may have resulted in an accidental death? But the authorities said there were no physical signs of a struggle on Zack's body. Hmm...So many thoughts running through my head. If only I knew the cause of death that would help me.

More of the guys started to join us at the meadow now, and I kept thinking I needed to talk to Tiny some more and see what other information he might have to offer me. He sure seemed to have a keen sense of what was going on around him, and I thought he might hold the key to solving this mystery. The mysterious scent of a phantom that night had me curious. Who was that sneaking around late that night, and what time was that?

Needless to say, I lost that game to Warren and he wanted to go best two out of three, but I convinced him to hit me up later. I wanted to chill out for a while.

Just as I stood up to walk back up to the gazebo and see if Tiny was in his usual chair, Russ sashayed right through our group with a "*...don'tcha wish your girlfriend was a lot like me, ...don'tcha wish your girlfriend was HOT like me, don'tcha, ...don'tcha?*" His antics brought a round of laughter from the guys.

"I'm going up to grab something to drink; does anyone need anything while I'm up there?"

"Thanks, Tony. I think we're good."

I walked up to the gazebo and grabbed a bottled water from the iced tub full of drinks and then pulled up a chair next to Tiny for a while.

"Morning, Tiny, how was breakfast?"

"Mine was good. How about you—did you enjoy?"

"Yes, very much so! The food here is good."

"It's not too bad."

"And I understand you're on a special diet for diabetes?"

"Not really. I'm not all that bad with it, but I do watch what I eat. Zack was the one that really had to watch what he ate and drank."

"Really? That must be tough to deal with all the time."

"I'm sure. And as I say, fortunately I'm not all that bad with it yet anyway. That's why Zack didn't drink alcohol either, I'd imagine."

"And yet they said he was drunk the night that he died?"

"Yeah, that's why that whole thing doesn't make sense."

"It does sound pretty strange, doesn't it?"

"I just have to monitor my blood sugar levels every day but Zack had to give himself shots daily for his diabetes."

"Really? That is pretty serious. So he actually injected himself daily?"

"Yeah, he would shoot up in the evenings some time after dinner and before turning in for the evening. He and I talked about it quite a bit because I'm probably looking at that fate some time down the road."

"Wow! What a pain to deal with all the time."

"Yep. And having to travel all the time with the medication and the needles and stuff. That is a pain.

That insulin has to be refrigerated, you know."

"I think I heard that at some time from someone."

"I don't look forward to having to deal with that, and hopefully I never will. If I can lose some weight, it would help me out a great deal."

"Well, I understand the kitchen didn't have a special meal prepared for Zack that first night. Do you think that might have affected his sugar levels enough to jeopardize his stability with his diabetes?"

"I guess it could have, why?"

"Well, I just thought since you never saw Zack drink alcohol that night, maybe his sugar levels spiked and caused him to pass out in the river and drown."

"Yeah. I guess that is quite possible, but Zack watched that pretty close. I guess it could have happened, though."

"Hey, guys, anyone up for a game of croquet in the meadow?" Russ approached us as we were talking.

The thought of naked croquet sounded pretty intriguing and, after all, I had just had my first naked yoga experience. I was ready to take my mind off of this whole thing, so why not. "Sure, I'll play, Russ."

"Good, I think we have a full game now. Oh, Tiny, did you want to play?"

"Oh, gawd no, Russ, but thanks anyway."

"OK, you can be the cheering section. Ha, ha!"

Six naked men gathered around the croquet set to pick our colors and I ended up with red. It was a fun pastime and by this time I was totally comfortable being naked around these guys. They were all so nice, and it was becoming so natural for me to function in a naked environment.

"Poison!" Russ yelled out first as he completed the course.

Oh my God, I thought. That could be it! That one word brought me back to Zack—and I now suspected he was poisoned somehow. But how and why and who?

Since there were no signs of bruises or scratches from a struggle on Zack's body, and if he truly was murdered, death by poisoning now seemed most logical. This could be accomplished in many ways and, again, an autopsy would show that.

After that interesting game of naked croquet, something I never dreamed of ever doing—but I'd never considered naked yoga either!—I wanted to take some time to chill out and try to gather my thoughts and analyze the recent information I'd collected. I spread out my towel in a corner of the meadow under a shade tree and connected to my iPod to try and sort this out in my head. It was not long, however, before I was sound asleep in the cool grass of the meadow under the filtered shade of an Alderwood tree.

"Tony, Tony, are you awake?" I heard a voice calling. I had slept for nearly an hour.

"Oh, hey, Eric!" I removed my ear pieces from my ears so we could talk.

"I was just up at the gazebo and was talking to Tiny and he was asking for you.... He wondered if you were down here."

"Really? I wonder what that's about. Did he say what he wanted?"

"Nope, he just said he wanted to talk to you when you get a chance and asked me to let you know."

"Thanks, Eric. I could use a bottled water anyway, so maybe I'll head up to the gazebo. I assume he's up there in his chair still?"

"Yeah, he's pretty much a fixture there."

"Thanks!"

"Sure thing; no problem. Later, guy!"

I thought this was very curious that Tiny would summon me, but there was apparently something he felt I should know. I didn't waste any time getting my ass up to the gazebo.

I grabbed a bottled water and walked over to Tiny.

"Hey, Tiny, can I get you a soda or some water?"

"Hey, Mr. Tony...no, but thanks anyway!"

"Eric said you were asking about me?"

"Yeah, I think I know why you were so curious about James and Zack, and I remembered something about Thursday night that I thought was interesting."

"Really?"

"Yeah...you're staying in the Alderwood campground, right? I've noticed you walking from that direction."

"Yes."

"That's the yurt that Zack was staying in. Are James and Cam staying down there also?"

"No, I haven't seen them in Alderwood. I think they're staying in the other campground."

"Well, Thursday night at dinner, I didn't go up to the cookhouse, as I wasn't feeling well that night. My stomach was upset and I chose not to go up and instead stayed here in my chair in the shadows of this tree."

"Oh?"

"Yeah, and I noticed James coming back from the Alderwood campground by himself while everyone else was up at the cookhouse. I thought that was a little strange, but he didn't seem to notice me and I watched him head back up to the cookhouse and join Cam and the other guests."

"That does seem pretty odd to me too. I wonder what that was about."

"I don't know—probably nothing, but I thought you might like to know, and as I said it's probably nothing at all, but it seemed a little out of the ordinary."

"Thanks, Tiny. I appreciate the information."

"Sure. No problem.... Oh, and Tony, by the way, I think I know what you're doing and I'll help you in any way I can."

**"Ding, ding...ding, ding!"**

What was it that Tiny thought he knew? I chose to

ignore the comment. "Time for lunch, Tiny. I'll see you up there. I need to grab my sarong."

"See you at lunch, Mr. Tony!"

# 10

## Invitation to Rendezvous

Here it was Sunday lunch, and I was enjoying the fellowship with all the guys and the nudity thing was no longer an issue for me. But I was here on an assignment, and I knew even though I was getting a feel for what might have happened, I needed some evidence, and things were all still very sketchy in my mind.

I felt I still needed to talk with Russ to find out the nature of his relationship with Zack. I knew there was a disagreement between them, but to what extent had that disagreement escalated? Had Russ become angry enough with his rejection by Zack to cause him harm, or possibly an accidental death and a cover up? I had so many questions that only Russ could answer, but trying to get into a serious conversation with him wasn't easy.

After lunch I set out on my mission, to get Russ aside and try to uncover his involvement, if any, with Zack. Leaving the cookhouse I walked down to the meadow with Frank, Cris and Michael.

"Hey, Tony, are you up for a game of cards?" Cris was trying to find a foursome to play.

"Sure, Cris, maybe later. For now I think I'll just veg out and enjoy the sun and the refreshing river water."

"Remember what your mama always said: Wait an hour after eating before going in the water."

"Yes, MOTHER!"

"Oh, Cris?" I wanted to hear from him on this. "The first night in camp, did you guys play cards up at the cookhouse gazebo?"

"We sure did, until about midnight or later."

"Was Russ playing with you guys too?"

"Oh yeah.... If there's a card game you can be sure that Russ will be there."

"Thanks, Cris."

I noticed Russ at a distance headed down to the meadow. You could not miss that body—very lean, tall and slightly hairy, an attractive man. And now with the few days of a suntan, and skin oiled down with sun protection, he looked hot!

I decided to try and catch up to him without any of the others around him. That was not easy to do with this group, but oddly enough, Russ headed for one of the several tree hammocks to crawl into for a bit. I hated to interrupt but I thought this might be the only time to connect with him alone.

"Hey, Russ, how's it going? Enjoying yourself and some R&R?"

"I needed this. Work has been stressful."

"Yeah, I think everyone is enjoying the week. Too bad it had to start out on such a low note."

"Oh, yeah. That was so sad. I was really enjoying getting to know Zack too and found him attractive."

"So, I hear he was a handsome man. Did you guys hit it off?"

"Oh, I tried to hit on him and hoped to connect, but he was pretty distant. Seemed to have other issues with a former lover or something. A torch he was still carrying."

"Believe me, I know how that can be. So Zack and you didn't get together?"

"If you mean did we do the nasty, that's a negative. I surely wanted to with him—he was HOT—but he got a little upset with my advances."

"Did you guys have a fight?"

"Oh, gawd no. We exchanged words in the bath house when I stepped into the shower with him and I tried to talk him into going back to my yurt with me, but you could hardly call it a fight."

"So he wasn't interested in that? Was he seeing someone else—is that why, you think?"

"Geeze, I don't know. I do know that he indicated this was a boyfriend from his past and he still loved this guy. I really didn't care anyway. Sounded like way too much baggage to me. I don't need that."

"Yeah, I know what you mean. Who needs it, right?"

"Say, Tony, how are you with photography? Ever take any erotic photos?"

Wow—where did that come from! I wasn't sure how to answer that one, but I thought it might help me to get to know Russ a little better.

"I enjoy photography and took some classes in college, but honestly have never taken any erotic shots."

"Oh, well, never mind."

"Why do you ask—are you wanting some photos taken?" I was hoping he was not referring to *me* posing for erotic photos and that his inquiry was for shots of himself.

"Well, I was hoping to find someone to take some photo shots of me for my web page. This setting in the wilderness is so nice for some naked semi-erotic or erotic shots. I have a nice digital camera that's easy to use and takes great shots."

"Sure, I wouldn't mind working with you on that, as long as you tell me what you want."

"Kewl! That would be great!"

I was thinking: How would I get through this without embarrassing myself if I get aroused? Of course since it would be just Russ and me, it could be fun and we'd be the only two who'd know what went on. Sort of like '. . . what happens in Vegas...stays in Vegas!'

"So, when did you want to do this?"

"I was thinking tomorrow morning if you don't mind, like maybe right after breakfast, around 9:00? The morning light should be good at that time."

"Sure, that would be great. Let's plan on it. I'll connect with you here at the gazebo and we can go out for a walk to find some good locations for shooting."

"Great, you're starting to sound like a real pro photographer."

"One question, Russ: Why did you single me out to take pics of you?"

"Well, you seem like someone I can trust to take this seriously and also, I find you attractive, so it would be easy enough for me to get into the setting and pose for you behind the camera lens."

"Wow, thank you. That's flattering and I'm glad you feel that way. I'll do my best not to disappoint you."

"Thanks. Now I'm going to continue with my hammock nap if you don't mind. Looking forward to tomorrow morning."

"Thanks. It's a deal. Enjoy your nap in the shade!"

My mind was now on our planned rendezvous for tomorrow's photo shoot, but I was pretty much convinced that Russ had nothing to do with Zack's death. He just didn't seem to fit the profile of someone who could commit murder, or wouldn't report an accidental death. Besides that, Russ was playing cards late into the night on that Thursday with some of the other guys.

The thought of an erotic photo session with Russ had me pleasantly aroused and I felt a tingle down below once again, and if I allowed myself, I could be pointing due north with little problem. But I needed to get back to the meadow with the other guys and see what other information I could learn from them.

It was rare that we ever saw James and Cameron in the meadow but I was pleased to see them sitting in a couple of beach chairs in the shade away from the rest of the guys. As much as I hated to intrude, I thought maybe I should be polite and venture over to talk to them for a while. Hopefully I could learn something more about them.

James was reading a book and Cameron was thumbing through a magazine. "Hey, guys. How you doing?"

They both raised their heads from their reading with a surprised look. "Oh, hi, Tony."

Cameron never spoke much and this time was no exception. He just smiled at me. "I haven't been able to talk to you guys and wanted to come over and say hello."

"Yeah, Cam and I spend a lot of time doing our own thing which we enjoy. Are you enjoying yourself, Tony?"

"Yes, very much.... So, James, do you have a stressful job at home?"

"I do, Tony, somewhat. I do a lot of traveling. I work as a pharmaceutical rep. How about you?"

"Right now I'm between jobs. Just recently got my hours cut and then got laid off from tending bar."

"We could use your services here for happy hour. Ha!"

"How about you, Cameron? What sort of work do you do?"

"I'm not working now. I live with James."

"Really? How nice. I'm happy for you guys. Have you been together long?"

Again, Cameron paused until James spoke up. "We haven't been together all that long—sort of newlyweds, I guess. That's why we spend so much time in our yurt. How about you, Tony? Are you single or is there someone at home?"

My mind flashed to the sight of Brad at the Park last Friday and I wished I could say he was home waiting for me. But this whole week was a charade, after all—why not make up an imaginary boyfriend at home? "No, James, I'm single and looking."

"Well, maybe after this week we'll have you married off."

"Well, guys, I'll let you get back to your reading." I could see that Cameron was reading from 'Men's Fitness' but I couldn't quite see what James was reading. "So what's that you're reading, James?"

"Oh, it's a series. Mark Manning murder mystery series by Michael Craft. This is his latest one, 'Bitch Slap.' I enjoy his writing.Have you ever read anything of his?"

Murder mystery, huh!..."No, I can't say that I have. I

might have to check it out."

"Yeah, you should."

"OK, guys. Enjoy your afternoon. I'll catch up with you later."

"Later, Tony!"

That evening when I turned in for the night, I tossed and turned. But...not because of thoughts of the murder investigation running through my head. Not even close! I began fantasizing about the next morning's photo session with Russ. The thought of the two of us naked in the wilderness together. With me rubbing him down with oil. My hands all over his body helping him get aroused for the camera. Russ, in suggestive poses. A close-up on his groin. Focusing on his hairy chest and tight pecs. A shot of his firm ass while lying between his legs. It all was very erotic to me.

The thought of it had me pleasantly aroused and I found myself with a raging hard-on. If I was going to get any sleep, I needed to take matters into my own hand— so to speak.

As my hand slid down my stomach, headed inevitably toward my groin, I pictured myself on top of him, straddling him, feeling him thrusting deep inside me. The visual in my head of his hairy chest in front of me and the satisfaction of his hard cock filling me brought me close to orgasm. With pre-cum now acting as a lubricant, I began to stroke myself, faster and harder.

I could feel it building up inside me and it wouldn't be much longer. Suddenly, every muscle in my body tightened. There it was—the euphoria and satisfaction that comes from climax. I felt the warm thick sperm shooting onto my own chest. With my eyes still closed, I could visualize the white drops of cream against his tan body and brown hairy chest. I sighed with a feeling of relief and contentment.

Now, I could fall asleep. But something was still stirring inside me. Tomorrow is another day!

# 11

# Erotic Photo Session

Monday morning, and I had slept well after fantasizing about Russ half the night. Now, I needed to focus once again on the investigation. It was possible that Zack did just slip on the mossy river rocks and hit his head and drown. That wasn't all that inconceivable actually. It's also quite possible he passed out from a diabetic coma due to an imbalance of his blood sugar and in doing so, hit his head and drowned.

But I was here to rule out murder. Or find a murderer! So who had motive to kill? James, for one, since he'd stand to lose half of all that he'd worked so hard to build over the years if Zack's palimony lawsuit was upheld by the courts. That could possibly jeopardize his job as well.

James had a good career as a drug rep and made good money, but all of that would be ruined for him if his ass was hauled into court and this became an ugly legal battle. His family is very prominent from what I'd heard and they'd likely be very upset with the media coverage as well, so I could easily see that James had a motive to remove Zack from his life—and from the face of the earth.

"Poison"...the refrain from Russ during our croquet game kept echoing back to me. Had Zack been poisoned? That aspect of the investigation by the police was never considered since the family refused the autopsy. That thought kept playing over and over in my head until it manifested into an obsession. And if Zack was poisoned, who would have access to drugs that could kill and the knowledge to know how the body reacts to certain drugs? A pharmaceutical rep, of course. James.

Then again, Cameron had a motive too, as a jealous lover protecting his man from this thorn in his side. But I'm not sure Cameron had the ability to pull off a murder. He seemed so dependent on James for everything.

I thought at one time that Russ might have gotten into a deadly fight with Zack but that didn't seem likely now that I knew Russ had an alibi playing cards that night. And as quirky of a personality that Russ has, I didn't see him being a malicious person.

As I lay there in bed realizing that the sun was lighting this small portion of the earth ever so gradually, I knew what I had to do. I had to call Vinnie and talk this all over with him. But one thing was clear in my mind: If we were ever going to determine the cause of Zack's death, we needed to have an autopsy performed.

Recalling there was only one area high up on a hillside where Eric was able to get cellular phone service, I knew I'd have to take a long hike first thing this morning. Vinnie was almost always in his office early, and even though it was only 6:30 a.m., I figured he'd be there already and so the office was likely the best place to reach him.

No one else was up yet in the campground, so I could sneak out without being noticed. I put on my hiking boots and stepped out of my yurt, and found myself once again aroused at the vision of myself being naked with the exception of hiking boots. The thought of it reminded me of a porn video of Al Parker I'd seen years ago that I'd nearly worn out from watching repeatedly.

I'd connected my phone to the car battery charger just in case I needed to use it, and so I had to make a trek back to the parking area before my early morning hike.

There was a lot of dew that morning and the air smelled so fresh and clean. Crossing over the river, I headed up the long steep trail that Eric had pointed out to me earlier. I kept my fingers crossed that I'd be able to get at least two bars on my cell phone so I could get a connection and hopefully be able to catch up with Vinnie. I surely did not want to have to make this hike more than once.

Reaching the top, I turned on my phone. Thank God,

a signal and three bars. Damn, that was good for up here! Now I hoped I'd be able to reach Vinnie and not have to leave a message for him.

"*Ring...ring...ring...!*" C'mon, Vinnie, pick up the damn phone.

"Balboa Private Investigators. Vince speaking. How can I help you?"

"Vinnie, it's me, Tony! I need . . ."

"Hey, Tony. How's it going there? Are you getting any work done with all those naked men around you?"

"Yeah, whatever. Look, I need your help on this. Please tell me that Zack's parents didn't have him cremated."

"Well, I really don't know...ah, considering their religious beliefs of no autopsy, I'd imagine they're going to put him in the ground in one piece." I'd almost forgotten about this religious belief of his family.

"Well, if they've already had the funeral, we're going to have to dig him up."

"Slow down, Tony. What are you talking about?"

"I have significant reason to suspect foul play. My investigation is leaning toward death by poisoning and there seemed to be a lot of hard feelings between Zack and some of the guys. If Zack was murdered an autopsy could prove that."

I was pretty excited now and starting to talk faster. "You need to file a 'Stay of Interment' with the Courts and stop the funeral plans if he's not already been buried.

Even if his death was accidental, due to a fall, an autopsy would show that as well."

"But the family did not want an autopsy on the body, Tony!"

"That doesn't matter. Legally if there's reason to suspect foul play and an autopsy will prove the cause of death, we can petition the Courts to step in. They'll just put the body on ice until a decision can be made. If he's already been buried, than we can have the body exhumed and the autopsy run."

"Tony, are sure of this? You know if we're wrong on this one, we're not going to ever live this one down and it'll be really bad for business—and your career."

"Trust me on this one, Vinnie; I have a strong feeling on this. I keep thinking 'poison' and the autopsy would show that."

"OK, let me see what I can do. I'll call the boy's parents and check with them on the funeral arrangements first, and find out what funeral home is handling the arrangements for them."

"Great!"

"Then I'll stop by the courthouse and file the 'Stay' and then fax a copy over to the funeral home so they'll stop all further plans and put everything on hold."

"Thanks. Then go ahead and order the autopsy and let me know how things go on your end."

"Tony, you know the boy's parents are not going to be

happy with this."

"Vinnie, they hired us to do a job, and if they want the job completed, we have to do what we have to do to get 'er done! Trust me on this one!"

"Let me see what I can do, and I'll call you back."

"You'll have to leave a message as there's no cell service here and I had to climb Mt. Kilimanjaro to get a signal. I can check later, but that of course means climbing this friggin' mountain again. I'll be anxious to hear what you find out on your end, and I hope you don't come up against a roadblock."

"Tony...be careful. Sounds like things are heating up there."

"If you mean the weather, Vinnie, it's plenty hot—was 98 here yesterday, but I think you mean getting hot in terms of danger—and that it is too. I'll be careful and I'll be in touch. Let me know what you find out. Thanks!"

"Talk to you soon. Bye!"

"Bye!"

While I had the chance, and the phone service, I thought I'd take advantage of it and check my voice mail. At this hour of the morning I knew none of my friends at home would be up yet or, if they were, they'd be on their way to work with the Monday morning blahs.

I had five messages and only two from numbers I recognized. One of those was Patrick calling me from Palm Springs—to rub it in, I guessed.

*"Beep...fourth message, sent Sunday at 5:45 p.m."*

"Hey, Tony. It's Patrick, and we're all here at the Barracks for beer bust and wanted to call you and let you know how much you're missed. Having a great time. Wish you were here. Hey, guys, say hello to Tony...Hey, Tony!...Later guy!"

That was really nice of them to call. I knew I wouldn't catch him up at this time of the day so I thought I'd best text him back.

"Hey P, thx 4 the call. Miss u 2 here. Hav lots 2 tell u when I get back. Ciao!"

I wasn't going to bother now with my other voice messages, but the fifth message was from a number that I thought I recognized.

*"Beep...fifth message, sent Sunday at 9:32 p.m."*

"Hi, Tony!"

I recognized this voice and my heart skipped a beat.

"It's me, Brad. It was good to see you Friday night and I've been thinking of you a lot over the weekend. I wonder what was I thinking when I told you I wanted to break it off with you. You're so sweet and we were good together.... Ahhm, I was wondering if you would like to get together for dinner some time this next week? Give me a call and let's see if we can set something up. Take care, my man!"

"My man." Oh how I wish I was his man. So here I was, unable to get back to him to get together for dinner and he's going to think I just don't care. Damn! The least I could do is send him a text message to let him know I'm out of town.

"Gd 2 hear from u, out of town now, but will check back w/u when I am home. Luv 2 get 2gether soon! Hugs, Tony."

Right now, I needed to focus and get back down to the resort. I had an appointment to meet Russ at nine o'clock and I still needed to grab some breakfast and then meet up with him at the gazebo.

We both walked up to the gazebo at nearly the same time. "Good timing, hey Russ?" I said.

"Yeah, I'm excited!"

I almost felt embarrassment for my fantasy with Russ the night before when I masturbated in my yurt. The scenario seemed so real to me after thinking back on it. He looked hot this morning in a pair of black jack boots and nothing else. He carried a duffle bag which made me curious. I wanted to ask him about it but I refrained as we walked off.

"So where did you want to go, Russ?"

"Let's head up the river. There are some great spots up that way, toward the swimming hole."

Little did Russ know that I'd just come from this direction on my early morning hike up the hill. As we headed out, my mind started to wander. What if Russ *was* the murderer and a psycho killer and maybe I was his next victim. Maybe he had a knife or gun in that duffle bag and he intended to kill me next. No one knew what we had planned this morning as we both wanted to keep the mission pretty hush-hush. Maybe I was Russ's next victim.

I couldn't take it any longer. I had to ask. "So, what's in your little duffle bag, Russ? Are you planning to get in a quick gym workout or something?"

"Ha! No, this is my bag of tricks!"

Now I was really beginning to wonder about all of this. Was I walking smack into a set-up, a trick that I'd fallen for?

"Actually, Tony, I have a couple of costume changes and my camera and a tri-pod in here. You know Cher has costume changes and so does this girl. There are a few other choice items too—toys that I brought. But let's not go into detail just yet."

Whew, that made sense to me now and made me feel much better. But then I started to get nervous about the sexual implications and I had knots in my stomach. I hoped I could really let go and get into this. Who knows...I might find a new career for myself. In photography I mean.

We hiked for what seemed miles but in reality it was only about a half mile before we found a great setting in the black oak trees with a rope swing and tire that would be a great spot for posing. The rock cropping here was good for some shots as well, and of course the water shots would be good once the jack boots came off.

Russ began to rummage around in his bag of tricks and handed me a very nice digital Canon camera and told me to look it over and see if I had any questions about using it. While I was doing that, he pulled out some body oil and began to oil up his naked bod. I soon realized it was the same scent that Tiny had smelled the night of Zack's death. Now I was not sure what to think about this mystery scent that seemed to be haunting me.

Rubbing the oil sensually all over his body was erotic and I began to get a woody just watching him. He stroked his penis with the oil and I watched as it began to grow. I grabbed the camera and began shooting, knowing there would likely be some good candid shots.

His first costume was a black leather harness to complement the black leather jack boots. This was a HOT look for him with that black studded leather against his hairy chest. I captured several shots while Russ made love to the camera lens. His next costume was a white jock strap with the boots and a football. While I snapped photos, he placed that football in some provocative positions which made for some erotic poses. That too had me aroused but I didn't mind that my erection was showing. That seemed to keep Russ aroused too, which was the look we were hoping to achieve.

Finally we finished off with some totally naked water

shots. I took several shots of him posing on the rocks and with the rubber tire swing. I zoomed in on his hairy buttocks with a fuzzy wet trail down to the crack of his ass. Finally, I couldn't take any more of the tease and I set down the camera and joined him in the water.

I walked up behind him, wrapping my arms around his torso. I grasped his muscular, hairy pecs, pulling him into me. I could feel his buttocks pressing against my hard-on. It felt good. His hand reached around and touched my thigh and I was electrified by his touch. He grabbed hold of my cock, giving it a firm squeeze. I could feel the blood pulsing into my erection. He turned and faced me, his fuzzy ass cheeks brushing against my hard-on as he turned. His mouth met mine and we kissed. He thrust his tongue deep in my mouth. I longed for his mouth on my cock. I felt my body growing weak as the blood now rushed into my groin. I grabbed hold of his buttocks and pulled him close to me. Our hard cocks rubbing against each other, the first signs of pre-cum now noticeable from the friction.

Over and over we let ourselves get close to climax, but stopped short, for what seemed to be eternity. We wanted to hold off with orgasm and enjoy this euphoria for as long as we could. Bringing our cocks very near ejaculation, then pulling back.... And then, we both could hold back no longer. In unison, we climaxed with an eruption of sperm. It was so awesome, and then...

we laid there in the wet sand on the beach in total exhaustion. Our bodies hot, sweaty from torrid sex and ultimate fulfillment.

How perfect was this. To enjoy a liberating outdoor sex experience in the wilderness – and best of all, he didn't kill me – at least not in the traditional sense.

## 12

# The Rattlesnake Incident

"Think we should be headed back?" Russ said to me, after our torrid sexual experience on the beach near the river, sort of a *"From Here To Eternity"* thing. We knew we'd have to face all the questions and jeering that we'd surely get from the others back at camp for disappearing for two hours.

"I think I have plenty of good shots for you to pick from, Russ, and thanks for the climax of the photo session – if you'll indulge me the double-entendre there, but I couldn't resist."

"Thank you, Tony. I'm very pleased to have so many great shots and I enjoyed our time together too. You're a very sensual and sexy man."

We started back down the narrow trail on the opposite side of the river. "Watch out for rattlesnakes. George said there are a lot up in this area of the river."

"Yes, I've heard that. Gawd, I hate snakes."

"Me too, and after the thing on Thursday, I'm just a little punchy now when someone says the word snake."

We continued on our hike back but I was much more cautious as to where I stepped. Even twigs were moving in my mind, now that Russ said that.

"So what was it that happened on Thursday? You didn't say and I didn't hear about this."

"Oh my gawd. That's right—you weren't here yet on Thursday."

"What happened?"

"This was Thursday afternoon just before the cocktail party that evening. I was up at the gazebo with a big group of the guys and I got up to go to the refrigerator for some more margarita mix."

"Yeah, so what happened?"

"Well...I'm standing there with the refrigerator door open and Eric comes up behind me and says, 'Don't panic—just close the door and step back. There's a rattlesnake at your feet under the refrigerator.'"

"Damn! That would scare the shit out of me."

"Duh, I nearly peed my pants! There it was, slithering at the base of the refrigerator. It looked like it was ten feet long but actually was more like three feet...but still a large friggin' snake."

"So what did you guys do? Was it rattling and ready to strike?"

"No. It was pretty content with the warmth of the

refrigerator motor and didn't look like it was about to go anywhere. Eric went up to the barn to find George. He's really comfortable with rattlesnakes having been raised here on the ranch with snakes around him all of his life."

"Yikes!"

"George showed up with a butterfly net and with the stick end of the net, dragged the snake out onto the concrete floor. Of course, that really pissed off the snake, which was rattling up a storm after that. Then, with one quick swoop, George had the snake caught up inside the net where it couldn't get away."

"So what did he do with it? Did he kill it?"

"No. He ended up letting it go across the river where there are many more snakes, from what George says. I guess they tend to stay on that side of the river usually. Oh, by the way in case no one has warned you, don't cross over to the other side of the river."

"Gee, thanks for the warning."

"So while George had all of our undivided attention, he of course wanted to show off a little. While the snake was in the net, he reaches in and grabs the head and the tail and pulls it out to show us all a little closer up. Freaked the hell out of me."

"Damn, I would've been out of there so fast!"

"He forced the mouth open so we could see the fangs close up and then he took a glass dish, sorta like a Petri dish, and proceeded to milk the snake venom from it."

"Yuk. That would bother me even to watch that!"

"Well, most of the guys were freaked out by it, but George was showing off for us. He finally took the snake down and released it on the opposite side of the river. Hope it stays over there."

"Wow! Sounds like an exciting afternoon. Glad I missed it."

"Yeah, wish I had. I was very close to getting bit by it and so glad that Eric noticed it."

"Hey, guys!" We were back at the meadow now and strangely enough there were no snide remarks or questions. I guess everyone expected us to hook up at some point.

Hmm! Something came to me and I needed to once again talk with Warren. He seemed to know Zack the best of anyone here. I knew I could likely find him in one of the hammocks in the shade so I set out to locate him.

"Warren! Hey! How are you doing?"

"Oh, Tony. Good, thanks. I was just about to doze off."

"Oh, sorry, but I won't keep you. I just had a couple of quick questions for you."

"OK. Shoot!"

"You knew Zack probably better than anyone else here and I wondered about his diabetes."

"OK?"

"Did Zack inject himself daily in the evening with insulin?"

"Yes, but what . . ."

"Please, don't ask right now. I just really need to know. So did Zack travel then with his syringes and insulin?"

"Yes, of course!"

"And that insulin needed to be refrigerated, correct?"

"Yes. Zack kept it up at the gazebo in one of the refrigerators. What's this all about?"

"So when he traveled, did he pre-load the syringes or bring the insulin vials with him?"

"Geeze, he did both. If it was a long trip like this, he'd usually pre-load the syringes so they were ready to shoot up. What's this all about? Why are you asking all of this?"

"Thanks. I think I have all that I need. I can't explain right now, but later I will."

Leaving Warren, I next wanted to talk to Tiny as I could always count on him to be insightful and forthcoming with some helpful information.

Walking up toward the cookhouse, I noticed Tiny wasn't in his usual perch, the Adirondack chair. Wouldn't you know it, the one time it was urgent that I speak with him.... I couldn't help but wonder if he might be in danger since he seemed to have witnessed some of what transpired just prior to Zack's death.

"*Ding, ding...ding, ding!*" There went the lunch bell—damn! This timing, however, could be good for me. I knew that many times Tiny would skip lunch, so maybe while everyone else was up at the cookhouse, I can get Tiny off alone and talk more with him about what he might have seen Thursday evening.

"Hey, Tony! You going up to lunch with us?" Cris asked from the crowd of naked men heading up to the cookhouse.

"Thanks, Cris, but I'm going to hang out here for a bit and might be up a little later."

"OK, but I can't guarantee with this group that there'll be any food left. Ha!"

I didn't see Tiny going to the cookhouse and was really beginning to get a little worried. Maybe he was up at the hot tub, which was the only other place I recalled seeing him hang out. So I hiked up to the sun deck and hot tub area.

I could see him soaking alone in the big tub as I approached. "Hey, Tiny, no lunch for you today?"

"No, I think I could afford to miss a lunch now and then. What about you?"

"No, the stomach is not feeling too settled this morning so I'm going to skip or go up later. . . .Hey, I just heard about the rattlesnake fiasco Thursday evening."

"Oh, yes. That was really something. I wasn't close by, but it scared the shit out of me. I'm very careful where I step now."

"I heard that George milked the snake venom from the rattler?"

"I guess that's what he was doing. As I say, I didn't

get close, but from a distance I could see he was doing something with the snake."

"And he had a glass dish, from what the guys said. The dish that the venom was drained into?"

"Yeah, pretty creepy if you ask me."

"Do you recall what George did with that glass dish when he took the snake down to the river to turn it loose?"

"I'm not sure, but I think he just set it down and then everyone followed him down to the river to see what was next."

"So you don't recall seeing the glass dish in the area of the gazebo later?"

"What's all this about?...Actually, I did see the glass dish. It was there during the cocktail party, but not sure what happened to it later. I assume someone cleaned it out or just threw it in the trash."

"Who cleaned up after the cocktail party?"

"Geeze, I'm not sure. I was kickin' back in my chair. I think it was the LIAHO guys that cleaned up."

". . . like...who?"

"Well, Warren and Art...and Cameron and James and some of the other guys from Santa Rosa."

"Then did they all go up to the cookhouse for dinner?"

"Well, yes, the bell rang while they were cleaning up and they all headed up to eat. I stayed around for a while since I don't like standing in line up there. I waited for the line to shorten up some."

"Did you see anything while you were here waiting—anything strange or out of the ordinary?"

"Well, I'm not sure...Tony, what's this about?"

"Trust me, Tiny, I'll tell you more very soon, but just humor me. Did you see anything out of the ordinary?"

"I think I know what you're getting at, Tony. As I told you earlier, I saw James walking back from Alderwood while everyone was still up at dinner.

"Do you recall his actions? What did he do?"

"Well, I'm not sure he noticed me in my chair but if he did, probably figured I was sleeping because he didn't acknowledge me at all. He got something out of the refrigerator, maybe a bottle of wine for dinner or something. After a bit of fussing around, he left—but I didn't see anything in his hands when he left, so I'm not sure what he was doing."

"Thanks, Tiny. That's very helpful."

"Sure, but . . ."

"One more thing. Did you notice if the glass dish was still at the gazebo when James left?"

"I don't recall, but I know it wasn't until some time later that evening that I noticed it was gone."

"Thanks, Tiny. You're the best. I gotta run but we'll talk again soon. Thanks again."

"Oh...Mr. Tony. One more thing that I recall that sort of seemed a little strange. It was late that same night and the lights were already off inside the gazebo area. I think they're set on a timer to go off very late. In the darkness, I saw a shadowy figure walk into the gazebo area and after some fussing around, he appeared to be stashing something behind one of the refrigerators. I just figured someone was trying to hide something from the other guests, but it did seem a little strange. I recall the sound of breaking glass and thought to myself that is not good with bare feet around."

"Thank, Tiny. That's great. You've been very helpful. I'll fill you in on more details later."

# 13

# Case Solved?

While everyone was at lunch at the cookhouse, I made my way back to the gazebo. I approached the large refrigerator and felt a rush come over me at the thought of what I might find behind it. I pulled it forward and looked behind only to find a dead mouse and some cobwebs and dust.

Maybe behind the smaller one. I then grabbed hold of the other refrigerator and dragged it out as well. And there it was. The glass dish, now broken in two from the impact on the concrete. I located a plastic bag in the cupboard and scooped up the two broken glass pieces so as not to compromise any evidence that might be on them.

Returning the two refrigerators to their original position, I took the evidence I now had back to my yurt for safe-keeping and then set out to find George. I had a few questions for him and also was hoping I could use a phone in private to call Vinnie.

Hiking up to the cookhouse, the guys were now finishing lunch and starting to return to their daily relaxing routine around the meadow and the river. I noticed Bruce in the kitchen so I popped my head in.

"Hey, Bruce, do you have any idea where George is? I was hoping to talk with him. It's pretty urgent."

"Is there something I can help you with, Tony? Is something wrong?"

"No, it's no big deal. I just wanted to talk with George if I could."

"Sure. Well, I think he's up at the barn in the office working on bookkeeping stuff. You can go up there and see him. He won't mind."

"Great. I'll do that."

I hiked further up from the cookhouse to the metal shop they referred to as the barn and walked in to find several old cars in various stages of restoration. The office was an interior room built in one corner of the shop. I could hear music coming from this room and figured George must be working inside.

"***Knock, knock!***" I knocked on the door. "Hey, George, are you here?"

"Yes. Come on in!"

"Hi!"

"Oh, hey, Tony. What a surprise."

"Sorry to bother you, but I have something I need to

discuss with you and it's important."

"Really? Well shoot. What is it?"

"First of all, after Zack died and his body was removed from the resort, what did you do with his belongings?"

"Well, I gathered them up and placed them in a box, figuring eventually his parents would be contacting me to send it to them."

"And where's that box now?"

"What's this all about? Why all these questions?"

"Please, can you just tell me where the box of Zack's personal belongings is?"

"It's just outside the door here—in the barn."

"Can I have a look at what you have of his? It's very important."

"I'm not sure I should be letting you go through his things. I think that's for his parents to do."

"George, we have reason to believe that Zack was murdered. I'm actually a Private Investigator investigating his death, and I've been hired by Zack's parents."

"Oh my God, no! That's terrible! I had no idea."

"That means that I've done my job then. Now, can I look through the box of belongings?"

"Sure thing. It's just right out here."

We walked out of the office, and in a corner to the left of the door was the box of Zack's things.

"The one thing in particular that I'm looking for is the insulin that Zack kept in the refrigerator up at the gazebo."

"Damn, you know I never thought to check for that. The thought never crossed my mind that he'd have anything personal left in the refrigerators. I forgot about his diabetic condition."

"I need to get back down there and look for his insulin and syringes. Hopefully, he kept the used syringes to properly dispose of them later."

"I can drive you down there on the quad runner if you like."

"That would be great, but we can't draw a lot of attention. I don't want the suspected murderer to get suspicious and try to do something foolish like make a run for it."

"You've got a suspect? Who is it?"

"Right now I don't really want to say but I'll keep you informed as I get closer to solving this thing."

"Sure thing. Well, I've got some bags of ice that I need to take down there. We could stop at the cookhouse and grab those and the guests would think you're helping me out."

"Great idea, George. Let's go!"

I hopped on the back of the quad runner and we stopped off at the kitchen to get the ice before heading down to the gazebo. Once at the gazebo, George made himself busy with the ice while I searched the two refrigerators. There it was in the smaller of the two—an insulated lunch bag, with several pre-loaded syringes and only one empty used syringe.

Once again I grabbed a plastic bag, and carefully placed the used syringe in it so as not to disturb any fingerprints or other evidence that might be on it.

"Thanks, George. This is what I need. Can you give me a ride to Alderwood campground to my yurt? I want to put this in a safe place."

"Sure thing, Tony."

After I had safely stowed the probable evidence I had, I wanted to contact Vinnie and let him know that in my mind I'd pretty much solved the case. "George, can I use the phone up at your office, or somewhere that I can have some privacy?"

"Not a problem. Let's go—I'll take you back up there."

It was now approximately 2:30 in the afternoon. I felt sure it was too early to have any word back on the request for an autopsy, but I knew we had to act fast on arresting James before he was on to us and managed to get away.

I called Vinnie's office first. "You have reached the Office of Balboa Private Investigators. No one is......" Damn. I'd hoped I could reach him on his cell phone and that he wasn't in conference with a client with his phone turned off. That's quite possibly why he wasn't answering the office phone as well.

"This is Vince Castillo. How can I help you?"

"Hey, Vinnie. It's me, Tony. Thank God I caught up

with you."

"I didn't recognize the number and the area code."

"That's because I'm calling you from the office phone here at the resort. I think I've done it. I've figured out the murderer."

"Really! Do you have enough evidence to bring him in?"

"I think so, but the autopsy will tell the full tale. Is that on track?"

"I was able to get all the paperwork filed and the autopsy is being conducted as we speak. The kid's parents aren't at all happy with us."

"I'm sure, but when we tell them that their son was, in fact, murdered and who did it, they'll likely feel some sort of satisfaction, I hope."

"So who was it and shall we bring him in?"

"Well, we can only hold him for forty-eight hours, so do you expect the autopsy results to be back before then?"

"I'm sure...I should have them early tomorrow."

"Great! The murderer is his former lover who's attending this week's event with his new bf."

"bf?"

"Boyfriend, Vinnie!"

"Wow! That makes sense, but how did he do it without the police picking up on it, or without any physical signs of a struggle?"

"I'll get into all of that with you later, and believe me I have plenty of evidence in my possession to prove it was murder. And once the autopsy comes back and we run the fingerprints, we'll have the final word on what the cause of death was and all the evidence we need."

"Great. So if you can just keep this guy there, I'll call the Sheriff's Department and have them pick him up.... Oh, by the way, who is it that we're having arrested—that would help."

"You know, I just know him by James."

"OK, James it is. As long as you're there, you can make sure to guide the deputies in the right direction. Stick by this guy and don't let him out of your sight. If he knows we're on to him, he may try to get away."

"Sure thing, Vinnie. I'll keep him in my sights and occupied until the sheriff deputies arrive."

"Be careful, Tony, and thanks. Good work!"

"OK. I'll be talking with you after the arrest is made."

# 14

## Arrest in the Cosumnes

After hanging up with Vinnie, I briefed George on what was about to happen and told him we needed to keep a close eye on James and make sure we knew where he was at all times.

Of course George was not pleased to have the Sheriff's Department out to his resort for the second time in less than a week. This sort of publicity was something he didn't need.

On our way back down to the meadow, George stopped off at the cookhouse to update Bruce on the latest development, while I headed down to the meadow to find James.

Walking down the path from the cookhouse, I saw Paul in the distance headed back to the campground. If anyone would know James's last name, it would be Paul since he took all the reservations for the week. "Hey, Paul!"

He didn't hear me and kept on walking. "Paul!"

"Oh, hey, Tony. I thought I heard my name. What's up?"

I caught up to him and we continued walking toward the campgrounds. "I was just wondering if you know James's last name or if you could find out for me?"

"Well, sure. I don't know it off hand because of so many guys, but I have a reservation list back at my yurt. I'm headed there now if you want to follow me."

"Sure, thanks!"

"So what's the deal? You seem stressed, Tony. What did James do—rob a bank or something?"

I debated on what to tell Paul, but I felt it would soon be all out in the open and I needed an ally to help me keep an eye on James.

"Well, actually Paul, it's worse than that."

"Really? What?"

"Yeah, you see I'm actually a Private Investigator undercover here to investigate Zack's mysterious death."

"Wow! I had no idea."

"Good. That's how it should be. Anyway, I'm convinced that Zack was murdered. If I'm correct, I think it was James who had something to do with it."

"Oh my gawd!"

"Yes. So I need to know his last name since the police are coming to arrest him soon. Hopefully, they're already on their way."

Paul started to thumb through the reservation list.

"OK, here it is—James Herota."

"Thank, Paul. Now, can I ask another favor of you besides asking you to keep this under your hat until after the arrest?"

"Sure, Tony – anything. You name it."

"Can you watch for the Sheriff's Department when they arrive and get them directed toward James?"

"Sure. No problem! We should probably get back to the meadow and make sure he's around somewhere."

"Exactly. I'm headed down there now and I'll see you there. And remember, not a word of this to anyone. We don't want James to be tipped off."

"Right. I'll be right behind you, Tony."

I hustled back down to the meadow. By now it was about 3:15 in the afternoon, the hottest part of the day. The river was a popular cooling off spot as well as the few shade spots in the meadow. After scanning the crowd of men, I finally located James in the water, just kicked back on a partially submerged rock. It didn't appear that he was going any place soon.

Entering the refreshing waters, I worked my way over to him. "Hey, James. This looks like the place to be right about now."

"Yeah. It feels so nice and cool."

Little did he know what was about to take place and that his jig was nearly up. "Mind if I join you on that rock?"

"Sure, no problem. There's plenty of room."

"The water sure does feel nice."

I made some small talk with James. All the while that James and I were talking, Cameron was in the water too, not far away and keeping an eye on my every move. He seemed to be feeling jealous and threatened. I was glad he didn't interrupt.

I knew I had to engage James in something he was passionate about. I began talking to him about national health care and how that might affect him in pharmaceuticals. That of course was something that interested him, and our conversation got very in-depth and detailed, and I had to act like I was very curious.

Fortunately, I didn't have to keep James busy for long. We looked up at one point, hearing a commotion from the parking lot. In the distance, we could see a couple of Sheriff's Deputies walking toward the meadow along with George and Paul. James said to me, "Wow. Looks like the police are here again—probably more stuff on poor Zack's death."

"Yeah, I would guess so."

I noticed George and Paul talking to the deputies and looking over our way as they walked toward us.

"James Herota?"

"Yeah, I'm James. What is it?"

"James, please get out of the water."

By this time the deputies had one hand on their guns

and indicated they meant business. My first thought was to get away as far as I could so as not to be in the line of fire should they feel the need to shoot.

James stepped out of the water without a fight and the Deputy in charge handcuffed him and informed him he was under arrest for the murder of Zack Roberts. Cameron had been in the water not far from where we were and suddenly he was struggling to get out of the water fast and took off running across the meadow. Being barefoot, he wasn't able to run fast or far before he was apprehended by another deputy. He too was handcuffed immediately because of his suspicious actions.

The Sheriff's Deputy, not even thinking about this being a nudist event, acted on instinct and wrapped a towel around James while someone else had already tied a sarong around Cameron. By this time there were nearly 40 naked men gathered around watching this scene unfold before their eyes.

James was finally getting himself together and started to speak. "I didn't have anything to do with his death. I would never kill him! For God sake, we were lovers! I still cared for him.... That Thursday night I left the dining area to sneak back to Zack's yurt to leave him a note. I wanted to talk to him later that night around eleven o'clock. I intended to go for a walk with him and get him in the water and rough him up a little to scare him, so hopefully he'd leave me alone. I never intended to hurt him too much. I just wanted him to know I meant business so he'd stay away from me and move on with his life."

Cameron began crying hysterically now, and it made me wonder if he knew more than I'd originally thought. James continued with his defense. "When I got to Zack's yurt, the note was gone from his pillow and he wasn't around. I walked just a few steps from his yurt to the water, and there he was, floating face down, dead in the river. I just figured he'd slipped and hit his head and drowned. I thought it would be best if I left him for someone else to discover in the morning."

With all of Cameron's hysterical sobbing he finally yelled out "I'm sorry, James! I am so, so sorry. I did it for you. I didn't want him to bother you anymore."

Wow, I didn't expect that! I made my way over to my towel just in time to hear my name called.

"Is there an Antonio Felice here?"

"Right here, deputy."

"Hi, Mr. Felice, I'm Deputy Moreau."

"You can call me Tony. Nice to meet you, and glad you guys got here as soon as you did. I was wondering how I could keep James busy without him getting suspicious, but I had no idea it wasn't James, but Cameron that we needed to worry about."

"Well, it looks like you did a great job here, Tony. Thanks. Makes our job a lot easier. We're going to take both of these guys in for questioning and booking until we have the forensic evidence we need."

"Glad I could help."

"Now in talking with your boss, Mr. Castillo, I understand an autopsy is being performed and that you have other evidence to submit to me as well?"

"Yes. I have that all back in my yurt for safe keeping."

"Yurt? What *is* that, I heard James make reference to yurt also."

"My tent or cabin. They're called yurts."

"Oh, thanks. Before I have you get that stuff for me to be tagged as evidence, can we sit somewhere and talk so I can hear the details of your investigation?"

We walked over to an old wooden picnic table at the far end of the meadow where no one else could bother us and the detective began to tape my testimony.

". . . James and Zack were former lovers, and after James dumped Zack, there were a lot of hard feelings on the part of Zack. He intended to go after James financially for his share of what they had owned and then some. James was not happy about this so after I eliminated all other possibilities, I concluded it was James that bumped him off. Now, it appears I was wrong about who committed the final act, but I'm still convinced I have the methodology figured out. Hopefully, I'm not wrong about that too—otherwise I'll feel like a real loser PI."

By this time we had been joined by Warren who felt he may have something to offer since he knew James and Cameron better than anyone.

"Both James and Cameron knew of Zack's diabetic health condition and his need for daily insulin," I said. "They knew that Zack kept his insulin and syringes in the refrigerator at the gazebo and when he administered his injections daily."

"Late in the afternoon Thursday, the resort owner captured a rattlesnake and showed the curious crowd of on-lookers how to milk the venom from the rattlesnake. He left that venom unattended and at some point later that evening Cameron, as it turns out, got hold of it. He replaced some of the insulin in Zack's diabetes syringe with the poison venom, thus setting Zack up to kill himself."

Warren spoke up, "That makes a lot of sense now, because Cameron knows very well how to load a syringe. He was a junkie several years ago and used to shoot up cocaine. He's been clean and sober for a long time now, but he'd have no problem re-loading a syringe."

"And with James's pharmaceutical background, you can see why I suspected *him* of this." I continued with my statement: "Later that night before Zack went to bed, he injected himself with a lethal dose of snake venom, and then headed up to the campsite to go to bed. On his way he began to feel feverish and light-headed so by the time he got to his yurt, and found James's note, he probably made his way to the river's edge to attempt to have the cool water bring him out of his flushed feeling. Instead he got worse and then passed out in the river."

"I'm not sure if Zack died from the injection itself or from the fall into the river," I said. "The autopsy will clear that up. It's possible the venom only made him sick and he passed out, and in doing so hit his head or drowned in the river, just as the coroner had said. The reason for his fall, however, and for his death for that matter, is that he was poisoned by Cameron with rattlesnake venom injected directly into his system.

"There are several witnesses here who you'll want to interview and I have a list of those for you, but I'm sure you'll want to talk to everyone in case I've missed something. I do have those items that I've carefully collected so as not to compromise any evidence on them. I have the syringe that I believe Zack injected himself with that evening and it should have traces of rattlesnake venom in it as well as Cameron's fingerprints all over it.

"I've also gathered up the glass dish which contained the snake venom after George milked it. It's now broken in two pieces after Cameron tried to hide it behind one of the refrigerators at the gazebo. That glass dish should also contain Cameron's prints as well as George's."

"Well, Mr. Felice, Tony, you do seem to have it all together even though you had originally felt James did it, and that is certainly understandable. The fingerprints will prove if it was Cameron after all. The district attorney will decide whether to file charges against James since he walked away from the body once he found him in the water and quite possibly Zack was still alive at that time. It's doubtful, but possible. I appreciate your help, Tony. I have your contact information from your boss, and someone will be contacting you for a formal statement. You may be asked to testify in court at some time as well. We'll be in touch. Thanks, again."

"Thank you, Deputy Moreau! Now, let me get that evidence for you."

# 15

# Returning Home

What a relief to have Cameron and James in custody now, but I knew there'd be a lot of unanswered questions that the rest of the guys would have.

"Bruce, do you think maybe we should get all the guys together so I can explain to them all at once what just happened. I know there are a lot of rumors and talking amongst all of them right now."

"I think that would be a good idea, Tony. I'll go ring the dinner bell and see if I can get everyone up to the cookhouse."

"That should work out. Thanks."

We gathered everyone together and I identified myself as a PI and laid out all the details as much as I knew for sure. The guys were quite shocked to hear of the murder and they had a lot of questions for me. I think the fact that I was undercover amongst them might have made some of them feel somewhat deceived. Hopefully this would not be a problem with the new friendships I felt I'd formed.

Ordinarily, having finished with my assignment on a case, I would be headed home. This time it was different. I was enjoying the vacation and my new social naturist experience. If the guys didn't resent me now after knowing my true identity, I wanted to stay and hang out with them.

"***Ding, ding...ding, ding!***"

For the second time that evening the dinner bell rang and this time it was actually for dinner.

"Hey, Tony...you joining us for dinner?"

"Wouldn't miss it, Cris. You guys headed up there now?"

"Yep...just need to grab my sarong and get Michael moving. Eric, you going up to dinner with us too? I think we need to break out that bottle of good wine you brought tonight to celebrate."

I was pleased that the friendships I'd formed with the guys hadn't changed after they'd learned my true identity and motive for being there. At dinner I was overwhelmed with questions from all angles of the dining table. Turns out, I had become somewhat of a hero in their eyes, but for me, I was just doing my job.

"So, Tony, now that the case has been solved, are you going to stay and enjoy the rest of the week with us?"

"I'm thinking I will, Eric. If you guys still want me around and if it's OK with George and Bruce."

"Great! So, Tony, when did you put all of this together and figure out Zack was poisoned?"

"Well, Eric, it was after a combination of information from Tiny, Warren and Russ as well as several other comments made over the last few days by the guys. I think Tiny had me a little thrown off track at one point when he talked about noticing a mysterious scent that Thursday night but didn't see anyone. I think he must have dozed off in his chair and the only one of his senses that was registering was the sense of smell. He told me about seeing James at the gazebo, but hadn't noticed Cameron. That was what started me thinking that James was involved, when in fact, he was grabbing a drink from the refrigerator after having delivered a note to Alderwood to Zack's yurt."

"As it happened, Cameron had had a massage that night, and the scent that Tiny noticed was from the massage oil used on Cameron—as he loaded Zack's syringe with the rattlesnake venom that he'd hidden earlier when they'd cleaned up after the happy hour party."

"For a while, I even wondered about Jake, because his statement about his arrival time didn't make sense, and because the mysterious scent – his Patchouli massage oil – was connected directly to him. As it turned out, I learned that Jake actually arrived at the resort on Wednesday evening, not Thursday. I guess he's not all that good with details but when you look that good, you don't need to be."

"Well, I'm amazed and had no idea you were undercover."

"Good. That means I did my job well. Oh, excuse me...there's Bruce."

"Bruce...I want to thank you and George for all your help and support in solving this case."

"No problem. We didn't even realize there was an investigation going on. I'm just glad it went as smoothly as it did."

"I wanted to ask you guys if it would be alright if I stay the rest of the week. I've been enjoying myself so much."

"Of course...not a problem at all. We'd love to have you stay."

"Kewl. It'll be nice to relax the rest of the week. Oh, and I'll need to call my boss in the morning and let him know the latest details on this end."

"Not a problem. You can use the phone here at the cookhouse or the one up at the barn if you prefer."

"Thanks.... You know, Bruce, it's pretty ironic that the first person I met when I arrive here on Saturday was James."

"Yeah, Tony. You just never know. '...*Still waters run deep.*'"

That evening there was a lot of talk around the campfire and the hot tub. I think the guys were excited about the thought of having been part of this entire process.

The next morning I was up early and had my first

cup of coffee poured before checking in with Vinnie. Since there was no one around the cookhouse this early, I decided to use the phone in the kitchen.

I called Vinnie's office knowing he would be in despite the early hour.

"Balboa Private Investigators. Vince speaking. How can I help you?"

"Morning, Vinnie. It's Tony!"

"Hey, Tony. I got the update from the Sheriff's Department after the arrest yesterday. Glad it went so smoothly."

"Yeah, it went pretty well. Glad to have it all over though."

"Oh, and Tony, for what it's worth, the autopsy results came back and it was confirmed there was rattlesnake venom in Zack's system, but no snake bite on his body."

"Yes! That's the final confirmation I needed!"

"However, there is more, Tony."

"Yeah, what?"

"The autopsy indicated there was not enough of the venom in Zack's body to be lethal. Zack was still alive when his body entered the water."

"Really?"

"Yes...and to make things even more interesting—get a load of this! – the actual time of death was determined to be somewhere between 10:30 and midnight. With that in mind, it's possible, although doubtful, that Zack was still alive when James walked away from him in the water that night."

"Wow!"

"Yep, and it's likely that the district attorney will file charges against James as well for leaving the scene and not offering to assist Zack, just in case he was still alive by chance.... And for not reporting the death."

"Very interesting!"

"Well, anyway, good job, Tony!"

"Thanks! And Vinnie, if you don't mind, I'm going to stick around here until the end of the week when this event ends since it's all paid for. Besides, the police may have some more questions for me later this week."

"Hey, Tony, you don't need to justify it to me. You deserve some down time and to enjoy the rest of the week. Sounds to me like you sort of got into this 'nudie' stuff, hey?"

"Well, Vinnie, let me just say it's a liberating experience and I've met a lot of really nice guys."

"Good for you, Tony. I'll see you in the office when you get back."

"Kewl! Thanks, Vinnie. Bye!"

"Later, guy!"

Early that morning, another key piece of evidence surfaced. Jake had been doing some stretching exercises in the meadow and walked down to the river to take a dip. There in the sand was a faded handwritten note—the one James had left for Zack the night he died. "*Zack, we need to talk. I'll be back around 11:00 tonight so we can work some things out. James"*

Zack must have taken the note to the river and passed out in the water with it in his hand. Eventually, it made its way downstream from where Zack's body was found. This too would be helpful to the investigation and to verify James's alibi.

I spent the rest of my week enjoying the sun, and fellowship with the guys, and loved every minute of it. I booked two fulfilling massage appointments with Jake, *without* Patchouli oil and enjoyed the touch of his healing hands. I needed that—and from such a HOT man, too.

Waking up on the last morning and gathering my things together in my yurt, I made a decision that I'd have never dreamed of making. I decided to find Paul and give him my reservation deposit for next year's MANS week at Rancho Sierra.

Having said my goodbyes to all my newfound friends and stowed my belongings in my rental car, the last thing for me to do before heading to the Sacramento Airport was to put on some shorts! I don't think they would like it if I tried to fly naked, although it would certainly make the airport screening process foolproof and much faster.

"Ladies and Gentlemen, this is your captain speaking. We'll soon be on the ground at San Diego Airport where the temperature currently is a comfortable 88 degrees. Please be sure your seatbelt is fastened, and remain in your seat until we have come to a full stop at the airport terminal. Thank you."

I was thrilled at the thought of being home and reconnecting with Brad. Perhaps we'll be able to rekindle that flame we once had. For me, that flame never went out completely and likely never will. I don't want to get hurt again, so I need to take it slow and see where things go with Brad and how sincere he is this time around.

I was also anxious to talk to Patrick and tell him all about my weekend and of course hear how the White Party in Palm Springs had gone. But I'm sure any adventures he might have had would pale in comparison to my week in the foothills of Plymouth at Rancho Sierra.

*"...Still waters run deep."*

# Epilogue

Zack's parents were grateful to Tony for finding out how their son was murdered, despite their resistance to cooperate with the investigation at the start. They would never, they later told him, have been at peace suspecting it was more than just a simple accident, but not knowing for sure.

James cooperated with the police in the investigation but charges were pressed by the district attorney since the autopsy found that Zack could have still been alive when James found him. Had he pulled Zack's body from the river, he might have been able to revive him. He got off easy, and was sentenced to one year in prison and six months of probation for not assisting a victim and for leaving the scene without reporting a body in the water.

Cameron, on the other hand, was found guilty of involuntary manslaughter and sentenced to 50 years to life in prison with eligibility for parole in 25 years. With good behavior, he could one day leave the prison walls, and try to pick up the pieces of his life. Tony returned to San Diego and was promoted to Senior PI. It was more than just a title – it was accompanied by a handsome raise as well.

With the solution of this crime, which came to be called the *Cosumnes River Murder*, he has become well respected by his peers and is well on his way to achieving his goal of some day owning his own Private Investigator firm.

Tony has continued to learn more about the naturist community and expand his circle of nudist friends. He now seeks out clothing-optional vacations and enjoys every bit of time he can find to shed his clothes. Weekends, he can usually be found at Black's Beach with the other nude sun worshipers.

His love life has its ups and downs, but he's on a high after reconnecting with his old boyfriend, Brad. They started dating again and life has been going well for the two of them.

In the next Tony Felice mystery series, you will learn more about Brad and Tony and their relationship, and how – or if – this romance progresses.

As Tony continues to solve crimes in the gay community, among his favorite memories will always be the week spent with MANS the year that Zack was murdered and found dead in the river at Rancho Sierra.

# Acknowledgements

I would like to thank all those friends and family that supported me with my debut as an author. A special thank you to Sonya Cox for all the many hours spent editing my writing and making me look good.

*And* . . . thanks for all the suggestions for enhancing my book from so many friends but especially to Cris Breivik and Mike Funke.

*And* . . . for making the first impression of my book so appealing, thank you to Mark Anderson for designing the cover, Kurt Kihlman for his cover photography and for his derriere on the cover, thanks to J Scott.

*And* . . . a special thank you to Palm Springs Koffi, south end for keeping my coffee cup full and putting up with me for all the hours that I spent writing this book at the coffee shop.

**Did you enjoy reading about
Tony's adventure?**

Want to read more?

Look for

# NAKED
# INNOCENCE

on Amazon

Book 2 in the
Tony Felice mystery series.

**www.TonyFeliceMystery.com**

www.ingramcontent.com/pod-product-compliance
Lightning Source LLC
Chambersburg PA
CBHW061137200626
46817CB00016B/1736